Hermann Lotze, George Trumbull Ladd

Outlines of Metaphysic

dictated portions of the lectures of Hermann Lotze

Hermann Lotze, George Trumbull Ladd

Outlines of Metaphysic
dictated portions of the lectures of Hermann Lotze

ISBN/EAN: 9783337423445

Printed in Europe, USA, Canada, Australia, Japan

Cover: Foto ©Andreas Hilbeck / pixelio.de

More available books at **www.hansebooks.com**

LOTZE'S

OUTLINES OF PHILOSOPHY

I

METAPHYSIC

THE editor and publishers of this volume beg leave to announce that two other numbers of the series of philosophical "OUTLINES" by LOTZE, viz., the one on the "PHILOSOPHY OF RELIGION" and the one on "MORAL PHILOSOPHY," may be expected within a few months. Should the reception met by these three volumes be sufficiently encouraging. it is hoped to publish the "OUTLINES of PSYCHOLOGY," of "ÆSTHETICS," and of "LOGIC," still later.

OUTLINES

OF

METAPHYSIC

DICTATED PORTIONS

OF THE

LECTURES OF HERMANN LOTZE

TRANSLATED AND EDITED BY

GEORGE T. LADD

PROFESSOR OF PHILOSOPHY IN YALE COLLEGE

BOSTON
GINN, HEATH, & CO.
1884

EDITOR'S PREFACE.

THE name of Rudolph Hermann Lotze, philosopher, has already been made familiar to a large
number of readers in this country, and no little
interest has been awakened in his opinions upon
various philosophical and religious themes. But
thus far the number who have attained any trustworthy knowledge as to what those opinions are,
has remained exceedingly small. Until very re-
cently all his most important published works have
been inaccessible to every one unable to cope with
voluminous philosophical German. Within the present year, creditable translations of the two large
volumes on Logic and Metaphysic, which constitute all of his System of Philosophy that the
author lived to publish, have appeared in England; and a translation of his Mikrokosmus (three
volumes in German) is promised soon to appear.
These works, however — especially the two former
— are not only large but technical and difficult;
few are likely to attempt their mastery who are
not already trained in the reading of German phi-

losophy. Yet there is scarcely any other recent writer on philosophical subjects whose thoughts are so stimulating for their breadth, penetration and candor; or with whom an acquaintance is so desirable for purposes of general culture through the philosophic way of considering life, with its interests in not merely pure thought, but also in morals, religion, and art.

It affords me, therefore, the pleasure that comes from the hope of being useful to a wide circle of persons, to announce that I have arranged to translate and edit several, if not all, of those little books called 'Outlines' which have been given to the public in Germany since the death of their lamented author. These 'Outlines' cover the entire ground of Lotze's mature teaching in the University upon the subjects of Logic, Metaphysic, Philosophy of Nature, Psychology, Æsthetics, Moral Philosophy, Philosophy of Religion, and History of German Philosophy since Kant. A word of explanation as to the origin of these books will suffice to assure the reader that he is to be put into communication with the thoughts of this philosopher in a way which he can trust both as to substance and form of expression. The German from which the translations are to be made consists of the dictated portions of his latest lectures (at Göttingen, and for a few months at Berlin) as formulated by Lotze himself, recorded in the notes of his hearers, and subjected to the most competent and thorough revision of Professor Rehnisch of Göttingen. The 'Outlines' give, therefore, a mature and trustworthy statement, in language selected by this teacher of philosophy himself, of what may be considered as his final opinions upon a wide range of subjects. They have met with no little favor in Germany.

I have used such competence and diligence as I could command in translating this first one of the Lotze series which it is proposed to publish. As far as seemed consistent with a desirable accuracy, technical language has been avoided, and the work presented with an English expression. Some of the terms employed in the original, however, do not admit of exact and elegant representation in our language ; nor has it been possible — had it been deemed desirable — wholly to disguise the savor of the class-room.

The Metaphysic was selected as the first one of the series for translation, because the views of the author on this subject were always regarded by himself as being, and in fact are, fundamental and initiatory to his views on all the other subjects to be treated. No one can make any progress what-

ever in understanding the philosophical system of
Lotze, or even in seeing the true bearing of his
observations on æsthetic, ethical and religious matters, who has not mastered his *metaphysical* notions.
This little book, then, should be regarded as furnishing the key and door to all the rest.

Two principal objects have been before my mind
as motives for undertaking these translations.   I
wish, in the first place, to further the work of
teaching philosophy by their use.   Such condensed,
orderly, and mature statements of conclusions on a
wide range of philosophical questions will be found
exceedingly valuable for both teacher and pupil.
They furnish a *scheme* for all the instruction which
the teacher is able to give in presenting and answering these questions.   When skilfully used,
they may be made to introduce the pupil to the
widest fields of philosophy under the guidance of
a great master, and in an interesting way.   They
present the applications of Metaphysic to art, religion, nature, and human conduct ; — and they thus
open regions of reflection into which the instruction of our colleges and universities scarcely takes
their students at all, — regions, however, which are
precisely the ones where such students both de-
sire and need to go.

I wish, in the second place, to have these

thoughts of Lotze do their legitimate work in liberalizing, expanding and elevating the culture of those persons who are wont to be styled the 'educated class.' Perhaps, since what is here offered to them is presented in so compact and manageable form, not a few will be glad to look on life, — in its widest extent, human and divine, — with quickened powers of reflection under the stimulating words of this teacher from another nation. With such an object in view, it may be regretted that the first number of the series should be the most abstract, and seemingly foreign to practical interests, of them all. But, then, as I have already said, it is introductory and fundamental.

It is not my purpose to attempt to defend, refute, or even characterize the opinions which these books will, for themselves, sufficiently set forth. Two or three remarks, however, will help to guard the uninstructed reader against certain misapprehensions of the author which might otherwise easily arise. The philosophy of Lotze is a remarkable combination of elements from the school and from real life. The elements which come from the school are both directly philosophical, and also only indirectly so through the physical and natural sciences. In the same year of his

life, at the age of twenty-one, he gained both the
degree of Doctor of Philosophy and that of Doctor
of Medicine. Although his earliest published
works were on Metaphysic (1841) and Logic (1843),
the first to be much noticed were those upon the
science which deals with the relations of physical and psychical phenomena : on the Physiology
of Life (1851) and of the Soul (1852). The thorough-going attempt made by the latter works to
apply the conception of mechanism to the phenomena of mind led many to misunderstand Lotze,
and even to class him among so-called scientific
materialists. The freest allowance is given to the
scientific conception of mechanism in this series
of philosophical 'Outlines.' But the reader should
never forget that in the view of Lotze, 'Mechanism' — or the coherency of the phenomena according to fixed laws of action — is only the means or
'way of behavior' which the highest Idea, the Idea
of the Good, has chosen to realize itself. And the
whole drift and aim of the philosophical system
set forth in these little books, is away from mate-
rialism. The disciples of Lotze — should he make
any among us — would become uncommonly at
their ease concerning the ultimate result upon our
fundamental faiths and aspirations, of materialistic
science and destructive criticism.

Some readers of the 'Outlines of Metaphysic' may be betrayed into the hasty conclusion that their author was pantheistically inclined. Such should remember that it is not the business of Metaphysic to go far in the personification of that Absolute Being whom it discovers as the 'Ground' of all reality, or in defining the true personality of the finite spirits which thus apprehend this Absolute Being. On such subjects, the 'Philosophy of Religion' and the 'Philosophy of Ethics' (Practical Philosophy) will give the elaboration and application of the author's metaphysical conceptions. It is my plan to have these two additional numbers of the series follow the one on Metaphysic, within a few months. In the meantime, if this philosopher also must be *classed* with others, let us affirm our hope and belief that his conclusions will be in the main acceptable to the many who are feeling strongly a certain most interesting and promising drift in modern philosophy. Among such are those who have learned much from Hegel, although they have been obliged to modify many of his views. The method of Hegel was, indeed, always opposed by Lotze; and he endeavored to make good what he considered the deficiencies of Hegel by substituting for a movement of Absolute Thought, a movement of Absolute Life, as the centre and sum of all reality. But, with all the differences in both method and conclusions of the two thinkers, Lotze teaches something like the same spiritual Monism as that into which many who have learned in the school of Hegel are leading the way. And for such as do not feel that they have learned, even indirectly, from Hegel the secret of reconciling science with æsthetics and religious impulse, Spirit with so-called Matter, and Mechanism with Idea, these works will be found useful in pointing out how a candid and well-furnished mind considered such problem of reconciliation, as well as in throwing light on many of the subordinate problems the solution of which is involved in the larger one.

It should be mentioned with gratitude that these translations have been undertaken with the kind permission of the German publisher, Herr S. Hirzel, of Leipsic.

GEORGE T. LADD.

New Haven, October, 1884.

TABLE OF CONTENTS.

INTRODUCTION.

— ·✦· —

§ 1. Our every-day apprehension of the World is pervaded throughout with suppositions concerning an inner coherency of its phenomena, which is in no wise immediately perceived by us, and yet is regarded as needing no explanation and as necessary. Thus, for example, even the most common apprehension of the world is impossible without articulating the content of our perceptions in such a manner that we assume 'Things' as the supports and centres of its phenomena and events, and all kinds of 'reciprocal actions' as being interchanged between them. Neither those things, however, nor these actions, are immediate objects of perception. In the same manner are both a theoretic apprehension and a practical treatment of the world inconceivable without the supposition of a causal connection of that which has actual existence.

All these and other suppositions we have become accustomed to in life with the feeling of their necessity, but without availing ourselves of a clear knowledge of their precise meaning and of the grounds and limits of their validity. There are therefore never wanting occasions where doubts at once arise in us concerning their validity. Thus in the consideration of human transactions, the new conception of freedom stands opposed to the 'causal nexus' previously deemed of universal applicability. Thus on consideration of the soul, the conception of 'Thing' seems to be in general inept to designate the permanent subject of its changeable phenomena.

These contradictions, in which the *extra*-scientific form of representation is involved, and to which the particular sciences also lead, — in so far as the axioms which some one of them follows in its domain run counter to those which another of them leaves undisputed in its domain, — make us sensible of the necessity for a universal science, which takes as the objects of its investigation those conceptions and propositions that, in ordinary life and in the particular sciences, are employed as *principles* of investigation.

This science is Metaphysic.

§ 2. The two questions that lie nearest at hand would accordingly be: How can we get possession of those suppositions *completely*, in order to have in collective form that total content of our reason which is necessary to thought? and, then: How can we demonstrate that these suppositions have any validity, or what validity they have?

As to the former question, it is well known that Aristotle first directed attention to those most general conceptions which are expressed concerning everything actual (the 'Categories'); but without conducting his search for them according to any principle, or giving any security that his enumeration of their series was complete. In more recent times, Kant attempted to make good this deficiency : Every act of cognition, he held, takes place by combination of ideas, whose form is that of logical judgment. If now it is sought to discover the different suppositions which we make about possible or necessary combinations of 'Things,' then there is only need to collect all the essentially different forms of the logical judgment, and it will thereupon be found that a special model of combination has been followed in each, according to which subject and predicate are thought of as cohering. For example : the categorical judgment ("gold is yellow") simply combines subject and predicate as thing and attribute; and this relation between thing and attribute is one of those suppositions which we make concerning the coherency of things. The hypothetical judgment ("if gold is heated, it melts") unites the predicate to the subject, not absolutely but conditionally; and the thought which lies herein, — namely, that of a combination of changeable phenomena according to a law of conditionating, is a second of those universal suppositions. Kant expresses them both by the brief titles of the categories of 'substantiality and of causality.' [In reference to this point it is common to remark, that the correct form, in which we are able to express those suppositions concerning the nature of actuality that are necessities of our thought, is without exception that of the proposition, not that of the conception. Only a *proposition* states a truth from which, by application to particular cases, definite determinations can be deduced. Conceptions are only elements which can form truths by composition ; of themselves alone they are nothing, until we are told what is to be done with them. It was on this account a hindrance to the history of philosophy, and led to inapplicable ways of speaking, that Aristotle reduced those thoughts to the form of fundamental conceptions ; and that Kant also, at least at first, represented the truth which is necessary to thought as a series of conceptions, ('pure notions of the understanding '). In a round-about-way he annulled again this deficiency, when he afterwards sought to deduce a system of fundamental propositions of the understanding from these conceptions of the understanding.]

On the whole, it cannot be admitted that this

clue, or that the series of forms of judgment to which it conducts, can lead to the complete, correct, and useful discovery of the metaphysical suppositions. Logical thinking is a combination of ideas according to laws of a universal truth; but these ideas do not relate to what is merely actual, but to all that is thinkable, even to all abstractions which can never of themselves have any actuality. The logical forms are, further, modes of experience, by means of which our human thinking combines and disposes manifold ideas, in such manner that a cognition of what is actual can be gained therefrom; but these logical forms themselves are not immediate copies of the combinations which take place between the elements of actuality. It is therefore to be expected, that this clue will indeed remind us of many metaphysical conceptions, because, of course, even that which is actual can be thought of only in the aforesaid logical forms; but that, on the one side, we cannot be led by it to all the fundamental propositions of metaphysic, and that, on the other side, we may by following this clue hit upon conceptions which have merely a logical value, and of which the metaphysical applicability is not clear.

§ 3. In the above-mentioned way Kant had discovered twelve categories, and, on account of the

consciousness of necessary and universal validity
which accompanied them, had considered them as
not derived from experience, but as an originally
inborn possession of our spirit.

Fichte took offence at the view that our spirit,
which every one inclines to think of as a unity in
the strictest sense, be supposed to possess twelve
different, isolated, fundamental conceptions; and he
proposed to deduce these Kantian categories from a
single original act or original truth of the spirit, as
a series of consequences, every one of which has its
definite place beside the others. Such original act
he found in this, that the spirit never merely *is*
(namely, as object for another observer), but continuously, and in all forms of its activity, withal is
'for itself' (*für sich* ist); that is, it knows, feels,
enjoys, or possesses itself, etc. ("the Ego posits
itself"). And now Fichte sought to show how this
'self-positing,' in order to accomplish what it wishes
or is obliged to accomplish, necessarily leads also to
the positing of a 'non-ego,' to the ascription of
quality to the non-ego, to the assumption of its
divisibility, etc.; that is to say, how the spirit is
necessitated by its original act to represent in general an external world, and to make, with reference
to the inner coherence of the component parts of
this world, those necessary suppositions which are
expressed by the categories of Kant.

§ 4. Kant had considered the 'pure notions of the understanding' as only subjective forms of cognition belonging to our spirit, and therefore as valid only for that which has once become 'phenomenon' for us, and not as valid for things themselves. But that such 'Things' in general exist, he had constantly *in praxi* assumed.

Even this the idealism of Fichte had to call in question : even that there are 'Things' appeared to it as an imagination unavoidable by our spirit, the external world as a mere product of a faculty of imagination working unconsciously within us. The necessity of explaining how different spirits construct pictures of the world that fit together so as to make one common world, led to the assumption of a single creative power, which, harmoniously active in all spirits, both images before them the phenomenal world, and also necessitates them to judge of this same world according to certain suppositions.

Henceforward this fundamental conception of an 'Absolute' determined the character of Metaphysic. The attempt was made to translate one's self immediately into the nature of this Absolute, in such a manner as to have a real experience of its developments, and not merely bring them to one's contemplation from without by the quondam means of human cognition, comparison of conceptions, and adduction of proof. In a 'dialectical method' (concerning which, further on) the means appeared to be given of beholding this self-development of the Absolute within us, in its simplicity and without disturbing it by admixture of subjective investigation. Schelling withal does not separate the two problems of deducing from this Absolute the general laws of all actuality and the definite particular forms of phenomena. Hegel designs at least to make this separation; and in his Metaphysic (which he calls 'Logic') he intends to depict that first inner development of the Absolute, through which it projects within itself those laws of every future possible world that are necessities of thought.

§ 5. Without passing judgment in this place upon the substantial value of the above-mentioned apprehension of the world, we cannot approve of the method it employs. For it takes its departure from an assumption (the conception of the Absolute) which lies very remote from the common representation; the content of which is very difficult for even the philosophers to define exhaustively; but the erroneous determinations of which become sources of mistakes in all subsequent investigations, — mistakes that are always the more hazardous, the more decidedly it is proposed to deduce the entire content of Metaphysic, in an unbroken series and without anywhere taking a new start, from a single principle.

Such kind of deduction appears to us the natural method of representing a truth with which we are already acquainted. Investigation, on the contrary, whose first business is to discover the truth, must take its departure from the largest possible number of independent, perfectly obvious and well-recognized considerations, with the proviso that the results which the prosecution of one consideration yields, shall be subsequently corrected, so far as is necessary, by the results of the rest.

In this matter, therefore, we esteem Herbart right, who assumes as many independent sections of Metaphysic as there are different distinct questions, problems, or contradictions, that meet us in our common contemplation of the world, and that are the separate causes of our philosophizing in general. For they compel us to attempt the reduction of the problems or contradictions given in perception, to one consistent, actual 'way of behavior' on the part of 'the Existent'; and, more precisely, to such a way of behavior as will withal furnish an explanation, how the appearance of contradiction cannot fail to originate for our point of view.

§ 6. That we are right in following Herbart in this matter is shown by the fact that the most differ-ent schools, however wide the other differences of their fundamental views and their methods, have, nevertheless, composed an articulated system of Metaphysic in quite analogous manner.

All these different schools experienced the neces-sity of discussing in the first place, in a section on 'Ontology,' (so the old Metaphysic and Herbart; called 'Doctrine of Being' in Hegel) those most general suppositions which we cannot avoid making concerning the nature of all things and the possi-bility of their coherence. 'Being,' 'Becoming,' 'effi-cient causation,' and such questions form the chief problems of all this section. They experienced

(2) The necessity of examining the forms in which the particular elements of actuality are united in one orderly totality. The intuitions of 'Space,' 'Time,' 'Motion,' and the most abstract of the cognate con-ceptions of 'the Natural,' form the chief points of this section, called 'Cosmology,' ('Synechology in Herbart'; 'Doctrine of Essence and Phenomenon in Hegel). Finally,

(3) They all arrive at the inquiry concerning the relation in which the objective world stands to that world of spirits by which it is apprehended. Within wider or narrower limits, the 'Rational Psychology'

of the old school, the 'Eidolology' of Herbart (doctrine of the forms of cognition), and Hegel's 'Doctrine of the Idea,' treat of the same subjects.

§ 7. The second of the questions adduced above (§ 2), — namely, How we can certify ourselves of the truth and validity of our metaphysical suppositions, cannot be decided previous to, but only in and by Metaphysic itself. For the bare question is without meaning so long as it concerns merely the validity in general of these suppositions; it interests us only so far as it touches upon the validity of metaphysical cognition in reference to an actual world, which we think of as an object standing over opposite to us. But the question whether such a world may be thought of, and how it may be thought of, is a metaphysical one. And as a rule it will always be found that those who, previous to the application of our cognition to actuality, are pleased first to decide the point whether it is thus applicable at all or not, judge this point in such a way as to assume ready-made a crowd of propositions concerning the nature of objective actuality, concerning the nature of the cognitive spirit, and concerning a possible relation of interaction between the two; while, nevertheless, it is only Metaphysic that can in the first instance demonstrate these propositions. The question which is disposed of unconsciously in such cases, we are going to undertake consciously; and we relegate it to the third principal division of Metaphysic.

FIRST PRINCIPAL DIVISION.

ONTOLOGY.

FIRST PRINCIPAL DIVISION.

—•—

ONTOLOGY.

(OF THE COHERENCY OF THINGS.)

—•—

PRELIMINARY REMARKS.

§ **8**. Metaphysic is the science of that which is actual, not of that which is merely thinkable. By *actuality* we distinguish a thing that is from one that is not, an event that happens from one that does not happen, a relation that exists from one that does not exist.

It is improper to apply the term 'Being' to this distinction; for this term, according to the customary usage of speech, designates only one kind of actuality, — namely, the motionless existence of things, in opposition, for example, to the happening of events.

Yet more hazardous are the designations of 'Position' and 'Putting.' For, since the very form of the word in this case indicates a transaction, these designations easily mislead us into the wrong course of wishing to understand or describe this transaction of 'putting' or 'positing'; or rather (as we choose to express the thought) of raising the inquiry, how 'actuality in general' is made. But no one can tell precisely how it is brought about that, in general, something *is*, instead of there not being anything at all; or how it is made possible that something *enters existence* through coming to pass, instead of everything remaining as it was of old.

This problem is not merely hopeless, but also contradictory. For every attempt to show how actuality originates, assumes the antecedent actuality of some conditions or other, out of which, or according to which, it originates. We can therefore never deduce all actuality, but always merely one form of actuality from another. And the problem of metaphysic is actually this: To discover the laws of the connection which unites the particular (simultaneous or successive) elements of actuality.

§ 9. If we summarize the most universal factors of the ordinary view of the world, it will be found to include the following suppositions: There are 'Things' in indefinite number; every thing supports certain 'properties,' and can, in so far as it has a previous existence, enter into all manner of 'relations' with other things; and these relations are the reason on account of which 'changes' originate in the things.

How much that is not lucid these suppositions contain, will be shown only little by little. At present, it is enough to remark that the two simplest of the conceptions here employed, that of a 'Thing' and that of its 'Being,' however lucid they appear at first, on closer consideration grow always more and more obscure.

While we require that the 'Thing' shall be thinkable *before* its properties, we, for all that, never achieve the actual thought of it otherwise than by means of its properties. While we further require that it must first 'be,' in order afterward to experience somewhat or to enter into relations with other things, we, for all that, never in experience find a 'Being' whose apparent rest does not itself rest upon uninterrupted motions and actions; nor are we able even in our thoughts to discover a perspicuous conception of what we mean by such 'Being' as this.

These dilemmas afford us the first materials for our investigation; more precisely, we treat first of the true significance of 'Being,' and afterward of the nature of that to which this particular species called actuality can appertain.

CHAPTER I.

§ 10. If the ordinary understanding is questioned as to what it means when it mentions something as 'Being,' in opposition to not being, it will without doubt appeal to immediate perception, and assert: That '*is*,' which may, in some manner or other, be the subject of experience by the senses.

If, however, we choose to formulate this expression exactly as follows, — 'To be' signifies 'to be the subject of experience,' — then this definition of 'Being' would by no means completely express what we actually mean by the word. For we ascribe 'Being' to what has been previously perceived, even when it is no longer perceived; and we consider its being perceived as only something which may possibly appertain to the thing in consequence of its unobserved, separate existence, but which is not identical with this.

In what now this unobserved 'Being' consists, the ordinary understanding explains very easily. While the things, that is to say, disappear from our perception, they still continue to stand in all kinds of relations with one another; and it is these 'relations,' in which, while they are not being observed, the 'Being' of things consists, and by which it is distinguished from 'not being.'

In more general terms : 'To be' means 'to stand in relations,' and being perceived is itself only one . such relation beside other relations.

§ 11. In opposition to the foregoing mode of apprehending the subject, philosophy is wont with great vivacity to explain : 'Standing in relations' can be asserted only of that which exists previous to such relations. Accordingly, the 'Being' of things can consist neither in their relation to us, nor in their relation to one another ; it must rather be thought of as a perfectly pure and simple 'position,' 'affirmation,' or 'putting,' which excludes all relations, but forms the ground of the possibility of becoming related at all.

If we attempt to think of this pure 'Being,' and to give to ourselves an account of precisely what we mean by it, then we meet with the difficulty of being unable to specify anything by which such a 'pure Being' may be distinguished from non-being. For if we actually exclude all relations, then the 'pure Being' would consist in a mere 'position'; by virtue of which, however, that which is thus existent cannot be discovered at any place in the world, or at

any point of time in the succession of events, and
does not assert itself in actuality by any effect upon
anything whatever, and cannot be affected at all by
any element of actuality. But it is precisely by
these same features that we recognize, as we believe, the non-existent.

Consequently, the definition, which represents
'Being' as 'Position without relation,' is so imperfect that it comprehends precisely the opposite of
that which is to be defined; it therefore needs correction.

REMARK. The purport of this conclusion is exactly the
same as that which forms the beginning of the Hegelian logic,
in the proposition: ' Being = Nothing.' But the succession of
mental operations which we have in this case accomplished
(namely, an attempt at definition; a comparison of the definition
arrived at with what we really meant, and the discovery of a
contradiction between the two; and, finally, a discernment of
the necessity of revising our definition), appears to Hegel as an
inner development, which was gone through, therefore, not by
our thoughts, but by their object: the Absolute, first thought of
as pure Being, is obliged to discover itself as such to be actually
identical with Nothing, and then, out of this unseemly identity,
to posit itself again by a new act of development in the new form
of ' determinate existence.'

§ 12. It will be objected that, none the less, an
existence, previously thought of in relations, cannot
by abstraction of these relations, pass over into a

non-existence; and that, therefore, the pure Being of the existence, which remains after this abstraction is made, is even still the contrary of non-being.

This objection is just only in so far as we doubtless mean by the term 'Being' that which is the opposite to non-being: we design to affirm and posit, not to deny and annul. But we are mistaken in holding that it is sufficient to consider this positing or affirming, intended by us, as valid in actuality, without concerning ourselves about the conditions under which these two conceptions have any applicability to actuality.

These conceptions really belong to the large class of abstractions which we correctly produce to aid the process of *thinking*, and which, in the process of thinking, we are also able, by combination with other conceptions, to convert into useful results : they are not, however, applicable at all *per se;* but they first become applicable to what is actual, when we attach to them again the abstracted correlates through which their meaning is completed.

Thus the conception of 'positing' is not applicable at all, if it is designed, without media, to posit merely something, and yet not posit it anywhere whatever. Thus, moreover, we cannot 'affirm' a Thing, but only a predicate *of* a thing.

'Pure Being,' thus apprehended, would therefore

be only the conception of an affirmation, to which must be supplied both the *subject* of which the affirmation is supposed to hold good, and the *predicate* which is supposed to attach itself to the subject.

It follows, accordingly, that, as was shown above, the 'Being' of things can consist only in certain relations on which the act of positing affirmatively falls, and not in a pure act of positing without any definite condition in which the 'Thing' was posited by the act.

§ 13. A further exception can be taken (so Herbart): If any existence, in order to be, must be related to some other, and accordingly pre-supposes this other, then a constant, durable positing of actuality can never come to pass.

This objection, however, confounds the useless question, how a world would get itself made, with the metaphysical question, in what forms of coherence can the existing world consist. And even if we should make a world, it would remain incomprehensible why the creating force, which we must then in every case assume and can in no case further explain, would have to be subject absolutely to the limitation of positing only one element at a time. But if we suppose that this force posited the entire manifoldness of the elements of the world, as related to each other, at one time, then the whole difficulty would disappear, and all the elements would remain constant; *although* each, — or rather, in this case, *because* each, — is related to the other.

Just as lacking in cogency is the other thought of an antecedent unrelated position, which is needed to make possible subsequent relations.   An element which were out of all relation to all other elements, to the world in general, could not even subsequently enter into such relation.   For, since it is obliged to enter, and is able to enter, not into 'relations in general,' but into certain perfectly definite ones, to the exclusion of others, the reason for this selection and this exclusion could be discovered afresh only in other 'relations' that would be already existing between the above-said element and the world. There is therefore no transition for 'Things' out of unrelated 'Being' into the condition of being related, but only an interchange of different relations.

§ 14. For the sake of explaining the world, even the view which seeks for true 'Being' in 'Position' without relation, is still compelled to assume that things do, as a matter of fact, everywhere stand in reciprocal relations; only — this Realism goes on to say — they are not so necessarily, but could likewise 'be,' devoid of all relation.

But the above statement means nothing else than this : There '*is*' actually nothing which does not stand in relations ; or, all 'that is' does stand in relations.   To speak, indeed, of 'pure, unrelated Being,' and at the same time admit that there is none such, means the same as to speak, not of the existent (which it is still necessary somehow to make good as '*existing*'), but of the non-existent, — something which this view considers possible, but which we consider a mere abstraction that has absolutely no direct significance with reference to actuality.

CHAPTER II.

§ **15**. If 'to be' means the same as 'to stand in relations,' then further inquiry arises : partly, What are the *relations*, to stand in which constitutes for things their 'being'? partly also, What are the *Things*, which as subjects enter into the relations?

The second question, to which from reasons of convenience we give the precedence, does not mean that the characteristic and concrete content of things is to be specified, — whether of every individual, in so far as they might happen to be distinct from one another, or of all collectively, in so far as they might happen to be of one essence. We have rather in this case to do only with the discovery of the universal formal predicates which must appertain to all that (whatever else it may be) which is to be called 'Thing,' or which is to appear in actuality as the 'Subject of relations.' In other words : we seek a definition of 'Thingness' (*Dingheit*).

§ **16**. The belief of ordinary intuition, that it has an immediate perception of the nature of things, can be only very short-lived. On closer consideration, it very soon learns : —

(1) That all perceptible 'Things,' although they first appear to intuition as undivided wholes, are composed of many elements, and that all their sensible properties depend upon the form of this composition, and change with it ;

(2) That the simple elements, in which we must now seek for the genuine 'Things,' not merely remain imperceptible, but that it would also be in vain to want to define their essence by means of other sensible qualities, since all such properties are dependent upon conditions, and, accordingly, cannot indicate the necessarily unchanging essence of the things, but only their way of behavior varying according to circumstances ; finally —

(3) That sensible properties also are not attached once for all, as changing phenomena to a single subject, nor do they proceed from it alone, but that they are always only events which are attached to the concurrence of different things.

For this reason, therefore, sensible properties are neither directly the content of 'the Existent,' nor are they phenomena which, although in an indirect manner, do, nevertheless, express the true nature of this Existent ; they are rather events which indicate indeed the fact and the manner of the *affection* or *action* of things, but never specify what the things *are*.

§ **17**. After it is obvious that no kind of sensible properties form the content of Things, we still do not need to resort to the desperate expedient of speaking of an existence that were absolutely devoid of content, and the entire nature of which consisted in indeterminate 'Being,' without any definite Somewhat to which this 'Being' appertains. The very name, 'the Existent,' by its participial form (in German, das Seiende) requires somewhat conceivable *in itself* which may as it were participate in 'Being.'

It would therefore be most pertinent, as a rule, never to speak of 'the Existent' absolutely, but always only of this or that definite existence. The first expression were allowable only on the supposition that the essence of all things be identical, and that there be, accordingly, only one existence, which just for this reason could be designated by the name of *'the Existent,'*—a name which in that case would appertain to such content merely, and to no other. The second expression makes it much more evident that just such is the content which must be pre-supposed as the content of 'Being'; and since it is attributed to whatever (no matter what else it may consist of) has the universal predicate of 'Being,' it does not include the pre-supposition—which it would be unjustifiable to make at this stage of the question—of the identity of all that exists.

§ **18**. Now since a content for 'the Existent' is indispensable, some persons recur to *Quality;* but, instead of sensible quality, to one which is *super*-sensible, which remains unknown, and from which as its later consequences the sensible properties are supposed to originate (Herbart).

If this assumption is not supposed barely to assert outright that the essence of 'Things' is unknown, then it can only design to assert : We know at least so much concerning this essence as that it may be formally apprehended under the general notion of quality.   The inquiry now arises : In what does the specific character of this conception consist ?

Without exception, the only qualities which are known to us as simple are those of sense, such as 'red,' 'warm,' 'sweet,' and the like; what we might designate as *super*-sensible qualities, — for example, 'strong,' 'pious,' 'good,' and the like, — very soon proves to be a form of representing the definite modes of the behavior of one subject under definite circumstances.   We can therefore merely form the general notion of 'quality' in such a way as to lead us to seek further for the universal factor of all sensible qualities.   Now since the classes of these qualities are altogether disparate, — warm and sweet, for example, having no common element in their content, — such universal factor lies solely in the form which our representation gives to them all.

The above-mentioned form of representation consists in this, that every prime quality is perfectly
homogeneous ; that in itself it furnishes no motive
for analyzing it into parts, or compounding it out of
parts ; further, that the parts, which the act of
thinking undertakes in an artificial way to discern
therein, are absolutely indistinguishable from one
another, cannot be brought into any essential relation with one another, and prove to be mere repe-
titions of our representation of the quality ; and
further, that on this very account, 'Quality' in itself
includes no reason for a definite form, magnitude,
and limitation of its own content, but must wait to
get this reason from something else, *with* which, as
quality, it is found.

In brief : All qualities are adjectives, and cannot
designate that which admits of being thought of
merely as a subject ('Thing'), but only that which is
merely predicate affirmed of another subject.

§ **19**.   To the preceding view it may be objected :
This universal 'Quality,' that we had but now in
mind, which is thought of as formless, and only just
qualitatively determined, is, of course, not as yet a
'Thing.'   But just as little must it be assumed as
though it were a kind of 'Stuff,' not yet cut out,
from which, by an act of limitation that is still waited

for, actual things are going to be cut out.   In actuality there is, from the very beginning onward, nothing but just these individually limited and definite qualities, from which only *we*, by our comparative thinking, subsequently form the abstraction of a universal, unmoulded 'Quality.'   And it is precisely the aforesaid limited qualities that are the things themselves.   To require, however, a demonstration of the way in which conversely 'Things' originate out of formless, universal 'Quality,' signifies only the renewal of the old senseless inquiry, how 'Being' is *made*.

Fundamentally correct, however, as the foregoing refutation is, it is not with it that we are concerned. For we are not wanting to know how things are made, but are only asserting that the conception of a 'Thing' is not thought in its completeness, when we simply think it by means of the two conceptions of an individually determined 'Quality,' and a 'Position' that rests upon this quality.   For mere 'Position' cannot make that upon which it falls into anything different from what it was in itself.   Even when posited through an unconditioned 'Position,' those qualities would always remain simply *qualities* posited, and would not be changed into 'Things' by the act of positing.

It appears then that the conception of 'Thing' is thought, in its completeness, only by means of three conceptions : namely, first, the conception of the before-mentioned *Quality ;* second, that of *Position ;* and third that of a *Subject*, of which the quality is affirmed by means of the position. This, as ordinarily expressed, signifies what follows : ' Things ' cannot *be* qualities, but can only *have* them.

§ **20.** The above-mentioned matter will be better understood if we reflect upon the following fact, namely, that we do not assume ' Things ' for their own sake, but in order that we may have them as subjects, — as the points of egress and of termination for ' events ' and ' relations.' For such a purpose a ' Thing' whose nature consisted merely in a simple quality posited unconditionally would be quite unsuitable.

We can divide all relations into two classes; first, relations of comparison, which originate at the moment when our perfectly voluntary attention brings any two elements, or rather their mental images, into a contact with each other that is quite indifferent and unessential to the elements themselves. Such relations — for example, ' similarity,' ' contrast,' ' larger ' or ' smaller,' and the like — signify nothing at all as to what reciprocal influences the things have. The second class, on the contrary, — that of objective relations, — expresses a proportion which is not

merely constituted between things by our thinking
in an arbitrary way, but which is really extant for the
things themselves in such manner that they are reciprocally affected in this same proportion. For example : The merely logical relation of comparison alluded
to above, — that of 'contrast' (of which, in itself, the
things that stand in it do not need to take any note),
— would become an objective or metaphysical relation, if it is understood as a resistance which things
really offer to one another.

Now it is obvious that only these metaphysical
objective relations are of any value with respect to the
essence of a 'Thing.' For everything that can be
conceived of at all, the unreal as well as the real, admits of such merely logical comparison.

§ 21. To such metaphysical or objective relations
as the foregoing, — that is, therefore, to being affected
by one another, — simple qualities are quite unsuitable.
For as soon as the qualities are *simple*, every change
of their content (and such a change is included in the
very conception of being affected in any way) completely annuls this content, and then an altogether
new content would take its place. This new content
could, it is true, when compared with the former,
appear to be connected with it by a definite degree
of similarity. But this relation of mere comparison

(by which even what is most diametrically opposite, even what is altogether incomparable, can be brought into a certain connection) does not by any means justify the assumption of an interior combining of the two in such a way that the second were a 'state' of the first.

The essence of a thing, if it merely consisted in a simple quality, would therefore with every change be itself totally changed; that is, a new somewhat would take the place of the old as it vanished, and the 'Thing' would have in itself no kind of 'reserve,' to which, as to its permanent nature, it could withdraw on the occasion of a change in its quality.

REMARK. The reciprocal effects which appear to take place in experience between simple qualities, everywhere go on only *apparently* between these qualities. Warmth *per se* does not change into cold *per se*; but only so far as the two are states of the same body, or of two bodies in contact, does the nature of these bodies carry along with it the impossibility of both states occurring together. 'Cold' is not in this way made 'warm'; but in a particular body the state of being cold is replaced by that of being warm. So that all action and reaction here depends upon the yet unknown nature of the real subject, and, on the contrary, only *appears* to take place between the simple qualities in themselves.

§ 22. To sum up the foregoing observations: The peculiar deficiency which prevents 'Quality' from

being the essence of a 'Thing' consists in its simplicity. Because of this simplicity, quality, on the
one hand, furnishes no inner principle of limitation,
and never forms a whole ; and, on the other hand, it
can only exist or not exist, but can never during its
existence be the subject of states of any kind.

We are obviously obliged to require a certain
'unity' of the nature of 'Thing.' Just such unity,
however, never appertains to what is simple, but in
all cases only to that kind of multiplicity which, by a
law of the combination of its parts, is so connected
as to resist every unregulated increase, diminution, or
change of its consistence, and to permit only such
change as invariably leaves the new state subjected to
the same law of its composition.

Passing over the further difficulties of this subject,
we express merely our provisional result as follows :
The essence of 'Things' is not simplicity, but the
above-mentioned unity ; and if this unity is to be
apprehended in thought at all, such apprehension
cannot happen in the mental form of the intuition,
the object of which is a quality, but only in the form
of the conception, the object of which is a law of
the combination of the manifold.

CHAPTER III.

§ 23. It is self-evident that, if we sought for the essence of 'Thing' in a multiplicity combined into unity, we did not design to consider this multiplicity as such, but only the *bond* which connects it together, as constituting this essence. On the contrary, it is well worth the trouble to inquire in what way it is possible to conceive of the fact that this bond, which proximately exists only in our thinking as the mental picture of the coherency of the manifold, is also really extant in the 'Thing' as an actual power over its properties.

§ 24. The doubt that arises next in order is the following : *Quality*, although in other respects insufficient, at least furnished us with an intuitive, concordant content as the essence of 'Thing'; but the conception which apprehends this essence as *Law*, makes it appear as though it were only a thought, which itself, in turn, is a net-work of relations between various points of relation. If quality, therefore, was too simple, then a law is not simple enough to form the essence of 'Thing.'

This first objection is not dangerous. For the compositeness and multiplicity of those operations of thought, by means of which we are wont logically to explain and to express the content we mean, is no proof whatever that the reality meant by that content is itself also composite. If therefore the essence of a 'Thing' were for us inexpressible save by many circumlocutions, yet it could none the less be a perfect unity, and need not itself *consist of* those parts, from the combination of which we originate its *expression*.

It will be objected, further, that a law appears even much less capable than a quality, of that reality which must appertain to every 'Thing.' This objection we might obviate, in so far as it is undoubtedly self-evident that, wherever we design to define in thought the essence of 'Thing,' the thought-image by means of which we make the attempt, must remain as a mere image distinct from the real Thing. Moreover, we can in no case give such an expression to our thought of the essence of 'Thing' as would be the real Thing itself, and not merely a designation for our cognition. And, finally, in every case, the way and manner, in which there becomes attached to this content of thought *in us* that actuality which makes the content to be a Thing *outside of us*, invariably eludes all our investigation.

§ **25.** Nevertheless, the whole matter is not quite settled ; but the question recurs, Whether a 'Law,' even if we think of it as actualized by means of an ever incomprehensible 'Position,' can in that case be a 'Thing.'

All that, to which we in other matters give the name of 'law,' is merely a valid rule, or a truth that prevails in the connection of our ideas, or in the connection of events as well. Of a 'Thing,' on the contrary, we demand a great deal more ; it is required to be a subject, that can fall into states, and be affected and produce effects.

Nothing of this kind, however, appears possible as occurring in the case of a *truth*, which is always valid, which always is what it is, and which, since it never changes, can never pass through any experience. Every such 'law' is rather comprehensible by us merely as that mode of relation wh' h flows from the inner nature of somewhat else ; and it is in this somewhat else that we are now looking for the true essence of 'Thing.'

In other words ; our consideration of what was meant by the essence of 'Thing,' leads us in a provisional way to the opinion, that the conception of this essence cannot be exhaustively defined without the use of three thoughts combined together : —

(1) The Quality of the Thing, that is, the law

considered above, or the *essentia* by which the Thing
is what it is, and by which one thing is distinguished
from another ;

(2) The idea of the 'Real,' the *substratum*, or
'stuff,' in which this *essentia* is coined, as it were ;

(3) The idea of 'Position,' by means of which the
unity of both the foregoing thoughts is formed into
the conception of *an actual thing*, in antithesis to
the bare *thought* of the same thing.

§ **26**. The conception of a 'Stuff' (*substratum*, ὕλη)
originates from the ordinary perception that a multiplicity of homogeneous parts, by diversity in the
mode of combining them, is fashioned into objects
of very diverse properties. Those homogeneous
parts therefore, when taken together, appear to us
as a yet crude neutral material, which is transformed
into products with definite characteristics only by a
subsequent process of forming. At the same time,
we know very well that this is only relatively true.
The 'stuff' is formless only in comparison with the
products formable from it ; in its own self, however,
it has a form which distinguishes it from other
'stuffs,' and is just as much a complete 'Thing' as
are those which originate from it.

On the other hand, the thought of a 'stuff' loses
all significance, if we are no longer speaking of

composite secondary things, but of simple primitive essences. For what we should consider in every one of these simple essences as the 'stuff' in which the characteristic *essentia* (by means of which one thing is distinguished from another) were actualized as form, would now inevitably have to be regarded as perfectly indefinite, as a so-called 'mere reality *per se*'; its whole nature would accordingly consist in 'Being' in general, without being anything in particular, in being affected and producing effects in general, without being affected and producing effects in any definite way to the exclusion of all others. That is to say: Such a 'reality' would obviously be only a logical abstraction, which could never have any actuality in itself, but always only in that from which it has been abstracted.

In other words: Reality means for us the 'Being' of a somewhat that is capable of being affected and of producing effects. Everything with which this definition comports, is accordingly called a 'reality,' —that is to say, has this title. But there cannot be a 'reality *per se*'—which were nothing—as the bearer of this title. What is supposed to be *real* must merit this designation by being susceptible, through its own definite and significant nature, of having reality in the meaning alleged.

§ **27.** After we find it impossible to distinguish in 'Thing' a kernel of unconditioned reality, and a form (*essentia*) attaching itself or given to this kernel, we are driven in the next place to the opposite view. This view asserts that the ever incomprehensible act of 'positing' (by means of which actual is distinguished from non-actual) does not in the first instance fall upon somewhat real of a universal kind contained in the Thing, in such manner that this somewhat real, by the stability now secured to it, acted as a *media* to provide permanency and actuality to the content also (by means of which this particular thing is to be distinguished from others). [It might, in fact, even be shown that it is perfectly incomprehensible how such a process could happen; and that all expressions of the kind — the content 'attaches itself' to the reality, or 'inheres' in it, etc. — are ways of speaking devoid of all specifiable signification.] On the contrary, the aforesaid act of 'positing' falls entirely without *media* upon the content itself, upon the *essentia* by means of which one 'Thing' is distinguished from another. But since this *essentia* is such that it, in its relations to every thing else, always behaves consistently in accordance with a law, there originates *for us* the unavoidable appearance of a reason for this consistency; and this reason being distinct from all particular properties and states of the Thing, and, consequently, also from the totality of its content, lies at the background of that content, — the appearance, that is to say, of an unconditioned reality on which the content depends.

§ 28. The second view mentioned above can be briefly expressed as follows: 'Reality' is that ideal content, which, by means of what it is, is capable of producing the appearance of a *substance* lying within it, to which it belongs as predicate. The manifold difficulties of this view must be postponed for subsequent consideration; in this connection we shall only bring to light the fact that this proposition needs supplementing in order to express, — not, to be sure, a specific conclusion, but, at the least, an accurate postulate.

If by the term 'Ideal' we understand such a content as (or a content, in so far as) can be exhaustively reproduced in thought, then such an 'ideal' (even if it be not apprehended as a universal proposition, law, or truth, but as completely individualized, somewhat like the idea of a definite work of art) would always remain a mere thought ; and, even if it were 'posited' as actual, it would not in this way obtain that capability for producing effects and being affected, which we are forced to consider as the most essential characteristic of 'Thing.'

We are forbidden, therefore, to understand the expression 'Ideal' as thus opposed to the 'Reality' previously referred to ; on the contrary, we must adopt into its signification the auxiliary definition, that what we so style has this meaning only with respect to *our thinking.* That is to say, it of itself, in a manner never demonstrable in thought, contains the aforesaid ideal content actualized in the form of an energizing existence ; but it does not owe this power of energizing to a real 'stuff' that is equally unattainable by thought.[1]

Therefore, neither does the reality precede its content ; nor does the ideal content, apprehended in a one-sided way as a *thought*, precede its own reality. To hold fast by such a separation of the two would only signify that we were, in our metaphysic, regarding the manifoldness of the logical operations through which we think of the Existent as though it

---

[1] Or expressed still somewhat differently : If we designate the essence of 'Thing' as 'Idea,' we must have regard to the two-fold meaning which the expression 'Idea' then has. For, of course,

(1) the 'Idea,' which we form from the nature of 'Thing,' is always a mere image of thought, which, even if thought of as actualized, would still invariably be only an existing thought and not an energizing 'Thing.' We mean specifically, however, by this word

(2) just that essence of 'Thing' itself which is never to be metamorphosed into thoughts in general, or quite exhausted in them ; and we call it 'Idea' merely because, if some thought-image of it is to be formed, it must not take the shape of a monotonous intuition, but rather that of a systematized conception, in which one law-giving formula brings a multiplicity of different determinations together into a Unity.

were a like manifoldness of processes in the Existent itself. Just as colors do not first give forth light in general and then (in the second place) become either red or green; and just as, conversely, red or green does not already exist in the darkness and merely become manifest by means of the light; just as little is there first a reality in the 'Thing' which afterward assumes definite form, or first an unactual form which is afterward realized by an act of 'positing.'

§ 29. In order to elucidate in some degree the meaning of our previous very abstract reflections by a concrete example, let us call to mind an idea which we very ordinarily are wont to have of the essence of the 'soul.' Since we only have to do with elucidation, it is left altogether undecided whether this idea is of itself perfectly correct, or whether it, like perhaps our own result as thus far reached, stands in need of a further correction.

(1) No one looks for the 'being' of the soul in an altogether relationless, self-sufficing 'position'; but the soul *is* only so far as it *lives*, — that is to say, stands in manifold relations, of affection and action, to an external world.

(2) No one looks for its 'essence' in a 'simple quality,' so that the true nature of the soul would

consist in this quality, while the entire manifoldness of its further development would only contain an, as it were, incidental succession of consequences, which would be wrung from this quality by circum-.stances.   Rather do we look for what is most essential to the soul in its *character;* that is to say, in that quite peculiar and individual law which appertains to the coherency of all its manifestations, — a law which always remains identical, while the occasions for these manifestations are variously changed.

(3) We have no thought whatever, at least in common life, of taking this personal character of the soul to be an ' Idea,' of itself devoid of all effect, which as pure form is attached to a ' soul-stuff ' that is in itself formless, but for this reason, all the more real.   On the contrary, whoever thinks of that character of the *ego* (or, more correctly, of that characteristic ego), believes himself therewith to be thinking of the entire essence of the soul ; — to be thinking, therefore, of that which, in itself and without *media*, constitutes the subject of all spiritual affection and action, and, accordingly, the reality of the soul.

CHAPTER IV.

OF CHANGE.

§ 30. If our conception of the essence of 'Thing,' —that it is an individual self-subsisting Idea—is, little by little, to gain the clearness in which it is still deficient, then the thought which manifestly lies concealed in it must first be brought to light: namely,—It is possible that any a may, under certain 'conditions,' assume a 'form' a, or a 'property' a, or a 'state' a, which it would not have without this condition, and which, accordingly, is different from a; but still in such manner that a, on occasion of this transition into a, remains identical with itself. We can call this in general the problem of change; and it is a matter of indifference for us at present, whether this change follows in time on account of the mutability of the aforesaid conditions, or whether a permanent condition impresses a permanent state a, that is different from its essence, upon the a.

§ 31. In the present case also we are to recollect that our problem does not consist in showing how, in general, a 'change' (if we think of it as in time-form), or a 'state' (which we may be able to think of as permanent, and therefore not in time-form) is *made*, and can be brought to pass. The attempt to show as a universal law by what mechanism in 'Becoming' the sequence of one condition upon another could be produced, or in what way that which we call a 'state' could be imparted to a subject in general, would very soon teach us that these questions are just as insoluble as the question, how 'Being' is made.

Our problem can merely be, to conceive of 'Becoming' in such manner—that is, so completely, with all the points of relation, separations and combinations of our particular ideas, belonging thereto—that the total idea of it is without contradictions and adequate to those facts of experience which we wish to designate by means of it.

§ **32.** Two opposite views attempt to solve this contradiction, — that, in changing, one and the same being is assumed to be both like and unlike itself, — by abolishing the unity of the being which passes for the subject of the contradictory predicates.

One view (that of Herbart and of physics) asserts that all individual beings, which are not already aggregates of others, remain perfectly unchanged; and that the manifoldness of varying sensible properties proceeds, for us, merely from the variation of their external and non-essential relations with one another (situation, position, combination and separation, motion, etc., of the atoms). The varying sensible properties, therefore, appear merely *for us* as a change of the beings themselves.

Nevertheless, it is very easy to comprehend that this theory, even when most strictly carried out, can only suffice to eliminate from all *external* nature any change in reality itself, and to reduce it to mere variation in relations; but that, on the contrary, an actual *interior* changeableness must, all the more inevitably, find a place for itself in that real being for which, as for the perceiving subject, the above-mentioned appearance of an objective change is assumed to originate. For in order that something may appear, a being is necessary to whom it appears. This 'appearing,' however, has no significance except that of 'being experienced.' Now, in order that the cognitive being may experience, sometimes a and sometimes β, it must manifestly pass over from one state, in which it previously was, into another, which previously was not. And we certainly cannot assume that this passing-over is only a variation in the external relations of this being to other beings, but that the being itself would be in no wise affected by such variation. For, in such a case, this being would not really experience anything, but would only appear to a *third* observer to be experiencing something. This, however, is contrary to the assumption ; for we wanted to know, how it is that anything appears to such a being itself, and not how it can seem to a second being as though something were appearing to the first one.

From what is said above it follows, therefore, that at least the percipient being must be conceived of as one that undergoes genuine interior changes, in order that the mere appearance of change may originate at all from the changeable relations of other unchangeable beings.

§ **33.** An opposed theory — that of 'absolute Becoming ' — tries to avoid the contradiction, while it altogether abolishes the real subject of change and maintains only a variation of phenomena, behind which no 'Things ' at all lie concealed.

Phenomena are, nevertheless, always phenomena *of* something or other, *for* some subject or other. The theories which make use of this expression have on this account, as a rule, come to the conclusion, not to deny all reality, but only the independent reality of individual things ; and to regard the latter as 'phenomena' of a single infinite Reality, — whether in the sense that this Reality causes the things to appear to us as objective, or that it, so far as it shapes also the nature of our souls, merely produces *in us*, in a general way, the idea of a world of things without its having any actual existence.

An actual 'absolute Becoming' would be taught only by such a theory as should assert that the actuality itself (not merely the phenomenon of an actual being) changes so that, in the place of one actual being which disappears, there comes another newly originated, without the conveyance of any reality, common to both and serving as the common subject of their content, from the first being over into this second. But such a complete discontinuity between every two moments in the world's course would be absolutely incompatible with thinking of this course as subjected to any 'law' or any 'order' whatever. For no law can ever combine necessarily what is subsequent with what is previous, if the previous state, which is assumed to contain the reason for a definite application of the law to the subsequent state, is so absolutely separated from this state that the two do not even belong to the same World. But that the course of the world is obedient to laws, — according to which it does not merely run on of itself, but can also, within certain limits, be changed by us at will, — belongs, as an associated impression of all our experiences, so much to the sphere of our most assured knowledge, that it would be scientifically insipid to examine further a theoretical fancy which is incongruous with it.

§ **34**. The conception of change in that which is real, is, therefore, not to be avoided. In order, nevertheless, to avoid unnecessary difficulties, we must raise the further inquiry : To what extent, then, are we under the necessity of requiring an application of this conception ?

Now in the actual *praxis* of apprehending the world, no one supposes that a being a can change without some principle of change and *ad infinitum*, so that at last it would become a z, in which no recollection of a is any longer to be discovered. The sphere of change is universally found to be limited in such a way that any a changes only into $a, a_1, a_2, \ldots$, any b only into β, β_1, β_2; and, in general, every real being changes only into such a 'closed series' of forms as, taken collectively, are deducible from the original nature of the being; while no being can ever pass out of the series of its own forms over into a series of forms belonging to another being.

Moreover, in the *praxis* of explaining the world, it is just as firmly supposed that a being a never passes into a new state a by its own agency alone, but only so far as a definite 'condition' X, that is different, however, from a, affects this a; so that, according to the law of identity, a in itself must, of course, always $= a$, — that is to say, *must* be unchangeable, — and, on the contrary $a + X$ *can* be $= a$, $a + Y = a_1$, etc.

§ **35.** Now, in the next place, this conception of change, when practically and actually applied, contains twice over a certain supposition of which we have to become cognizant.

That is to say, first, when we assert that every being is developed only into such forms as can flow 'by way of consequence' from its own nature, and never into other forms, then we manifestly consider all the thinkable predicates, which admit of being represented as future forms of whatsoever beings, to be cohering members of a single system comprising everything thinkable; and we do this in such a manner that each thing, as a member of this system, possesses a definite degree of relationship to, or a definite magnitude of difference from, all the other members. For only thus is there any meaning to the statement, that some forms, a, a_1, . . ., take their rise from a 'by way of consequence'; while other forms, β, β_1, . . ., could proceed from a only in an *in*consequent way, and, therefore, in this case, not at all.

Secondly: when we make the 'conditions' affect a so that different changes of a correspond to different conditions, we likewise assert, not merely that these conditions, $X, Y, \ldots$, must be comparable with each other, but also that there must exist among them such a comparableness to the nature of a and the nature of $a, a_1, \ldots$, as makes it possible that, in general, something follows from the conditions; and that, by way of consequence, there follows from one condition something different from that which follows from the rest.

After this supposition is once expressed, it appears trivial for the reason that it actually lies at the foundation of our entire consideration of the world from its very beginning. Since it contains no contradiction, there is nothing in it to correct; but it suffices to become cognizant of it, and to comprehend that it forbids every attempt to think of the essence of a 'Thing' as a *unicum*, such as were quite incommensurable with other things. The rather would an intelligence, which completely penetrated this essence, be able to apprehend it every time by a combination of such 'elements of the thinkable' — that is, of such predicates — as appertain, not merely to this one, but also to other things.

§ 36. The conception of change is, nevertheless, distinguished further from the mere conception of a series whose members can be deduced from one another in thought.

That is to say, the more such a comparableness of all that is thinkable is conceded, the more easily must different forms permit of being arranged so that some of them can be regarded as proceeding from the others according to a definite law ; and the latter again, in inverse order, from the former. Thus every member in a series of numbers depends upon every other, at pleasure. None of these members however actually originates from any other ; and, likewise, in the whole series of them no change takes place that invariably presupposes a subject subsisting through all the members of the series. On the contrary, there takes place only a succession of forms that are indeed comparable, but independent, and that do not come into existence one from the other.

In 'change' all members of the series are to be regarded as 'states' of one and the same abiding reality, and it is just in this way that there arises in the conception of change the contradiction which is foreign to the mere conception of a series ; namely, how this reality can remain identical while it is passing out of one state into the others.

But at this point we raise the inquiry, whether
this entire assertion of the identity of the ' Real ' with
itself during its changes does not belong to those
exaggerations which are discoverable in the abstract
conception of change, but not in its actual application to the *praxis* of explaining the World. Why
should we not rather admit that a, when it passes
over into a, does not remain identical, but is itself
really changed. As soon as we assume that such
change takes place by means of a condition X, and
that the a must uniformly be transformed back again
into a by means of an opposite condition $-X$, then
we have in this form of representation all that we
need in order to comprehend the actual change of
things in experience. It is not necessary that a
reality a remain uniformly $=$ a, and that it assume
a, a_1, . . ., merely as its ' states,' (a way of speaking,
from which nothing whatever can be gathered as to
the actual transaction whose nature it should describe) ; on the contrary, it suffices that a, while it
is continuously changing, remain always within a
' closed series ' of forms, every one of which can be
transformed by means of definite conditions into
every other, and no one of which can be transformed
by means of any condition into any form foreign to
this entire series.

This conception of a *constancy* or fixed connection

of antecedent and consequent (*Consequenz*) we, therefore, substitute for the unserviceable conception of
a complete identity of the same reality with itself
during its changes.

§ **37.** The other thought which lay in the conception of change, —namely, that a does not pass over
into α unconditionally, but only under some definite
condition, **X**, — calls for still further deliberation.
The question is, what is meant when it is said: a is
'conditioned' by **X**.

The above expression is clear to us only in the
sense that, if we in our consciousness place the
representation of **a** in relation with the representation of **X**, and compare the two, then there arises
the mental necessity of conceiving of the third representation α. The significance of this is: the content of α, for our thinking, has its underlying reason
in a combination of a and **X**. But in all change of
what is 'real,' it is not merely the *conception* of the
subsequent state which depends upon the content
of a condition, as one mathematical proposition may
depend upon a substitution which is introduced into
another; but the state α is produced, by means of
another state and by means of the condition affect-
ing it, as an *actual* state, — it having been previously
without any actual existence.

Now, in actuality, nothing but 'Things' and their relations exists. If, therefore, a condition is to be discovered, under which not merely thoughts result from thoughts, but actualities from actualities, then this condition must lie in some relation or other, which occurs between two or more things after having previously not taken place. The inquiry now arises, in what way the natures of these different things can become reasons for change in one another; that is to say, how one 'Thing' has an effect upon the other.

CHAPTER V.

OF CAUSES AND EFFECTS.

§ 38. From the repeated succession of single events ordinary reflection develops the idea of an inner connection between them, which furnishes the reason for this succession in time, and which as it is frequently generalized, expresses this idea as follows : ' Everything has a cause.'

The above-mentioned proposition is exaggerated. For not merely are valid truths like those of mathematics, — even when a reason can be discovered from which insight into them is gained, — produced by no 'cause'; but not even everything actual requires an act of causation. It is only the *change* of something actual that requires this. The 'Being' of an existence can in itself be regarded as perfectly unconditioned and eternal. It is only the special nature of what exists, that can, on manifold other grounds, excite a doubt respecting its unconditioned existence and an inquiry after its origin. Even such an investigation, however, must terminate in the recognition of some unconditioned being or other. And the well-known infinite regression, following which, every cause pre-supposes a new cause, is nothing but the token of a mistakable. use of the conception of 'condition.'

§ **39.** It is, further, incorrect to say that every-thing has one cause. This expression gives the appearance of speaking as though one being suffices by its own agency to produce the effect 'ready-made,' and then somehow merely transport it to a second being as into an empty space.

In the actual application of the causal conception we do not perpetrate this error : on the contrary, we are persuaded that the effect which a being **a** exer-cises, never occurs at all without a relation **X** in which it stands to a second being **b**; and that this effect, therefore, does not depend on the *discretion* of **a**, but *can* be exercised by it only under the con-dition of this relation, and, when the condition is fulfilled, *must* be exercised.

We further know that the effect of **a** is different according as it stands in the same relation **X** either to **b** or to **c, d,** . . . ; and that it therefore depends just as much upon the nature of the being (**b, c,** . . .) which appears to us to be the 'passive object,' as upon the nature of that (**a**) which we style 'efficient cause.'

And not less do we know that the effect, even between the same beings **a** and **b**, is different according as they stand in the relation **X** or in the other relation **Y**; and, further, that in every case the changes of the effect depend, according to a universal law, upon the changes or varieties of the things **a, b, c, d,** . . . and the relations **X, Y, Z.**

Finally, the effect produced will itself constantly consist in a change of both co-operating things (causes), and, likewise, in a change of their relation: that is to say, it will be a 'reciprocal effect.'

§ **40.** The ordinary usage of speech does not accurately correspond to that behavior of 'Things' described above as metaphysical.

Very frequently the reason (Grund) for the entire form of the subsequent effect (e.g., vegetation) lies in one co-operating cause (a kernel of grain), and the other causes (water, warmth, etc.) only furnish besides a condition which is necessary in order to give physical reality to this effect thus provided with a reason. According as one regards the work done in primarily fixing the form or in its subsequent actualization to be the greater, one will sometimes designate the kernel of grain alone as the 'cause' of the growth, and water and warmth, etc., only as vital 'stimuli'; or just the reverse, will designate the latter alone as causes of the plant-life, and the kernel of grain merely as the 'passive object' of their efficient causation.

And, further, it is very frequently discovered that the entire effect is perceptible only as a change in a single element ; while in some other element no effect is perceptible, although this, too, is really changed.   In such a case, the latter is wont to be designated as the 'active subject,' the former as the 'passive object.'

All the foregoing expressions, accurately taken, are untrue ; they are to be interpreted in accordance with the remarks above.

§ 41. If by 'effect' we understand the actual occurrence of a fixed event, then the explanation of it is twofold : the *content* of this event, by means of which it is distinguished from other events, and its *actuality*.

The aforesaid 'content' we understand as the result necessarily to be deduced, according to laws of universal verity, from those fixed relations between a and b that form the sufficient reason for this result ; and on this point there is in general nothing further to add.   On the contrary, even if this 'reason ' — namely, the relation X between a and b — enables us to understand why only the effect E, and not some other effect F, can proceed from the reason ; still we do not on this account understand besides how anything at all can

originate from that **X**. That is to say : An event **E**,
the reason for which, so far as its content is concerned, is completely provided in certain relations of
things, does not appear to be obliged to take place
and to occur in actuality, on that account alone ;
but such an event, if nothing additional occurred,
would remain continually unactualized to all eternity, as a result impending, necessary, and bound
to be. A special impulse, a '*complementum possi-
bilitatis*,' appears necessary before this event, the
reason for which is already complete, can be actualized.

The above-mentioned appearance is not contra-
dicted with perfect success by asserting that every
event, the reason for which is made fully complete,
takes place immediately ; and that where, in experience, such occurrence appears to be delayed, we
invariably find some insignificant part lacking to its
complete reason. It is through the addition of this
part which supplies the deficient reason, and not
through the addition of a special impulse of actualization to the reason, already complete, that the impending event becomes one actually occurring. For
all the examples which experience offers us, of delay
in the occurrence of an effect, do without doubt
admit of such explanation ; but this is just because,
in a way which is not yet clear to us, the matter, in

fact, stands as follows. The 'complete reason' for the content of an event (by means of which it is distinguished from other events) always includes likewise the 'complete reason' for the actualization of the same event, as soon as the aforesaid reason of the content is not merely thought of, but is itself actual as a state of this thing and of that other thing, and as a relation between them both.

At this point the problem presents itself: To comprehend why it is that this fact of the actual co-existence of two different things and of the above-mentioned relation, can include the reason for the actual occurrence of what appears to our thought as a consequence necessarily to be inferred from this fact. That is to say: We wish to know, how the aforesaid 'Things' can 'act' on one another.

§ 42. The ordinary opinion at this point tells us of the 'passing-over' of an 'influence' from one element to the other (*Causa transiens, Influxus physicus*), and thinks to see herein the process of efficient causation.

But it is neither possible accurately to define that which is here assumed to 'pass-over'; nor, if this could be done, to make intelligible from it the act of causation.

For, in the first place, if we consider what 'passes

over' to be a real element c, which separates itself
from the real element a, and 'passes over' to another element b; then this is, to be sure, a possible
form of representation, and, in fact, many apparent
effects produced by the natural elements on each
other depend upon this way of behavior. But in
such cases, seriously speaking, no efficient causation
is present. When water (c), for example, with all its
properties passes over from a to b, the only effect
produced is that these properties now appear at the
place b (which becomes moist), and vanish at the
place a (which dries off). If, however, that which
passes over is assumed to be not a real element, but
—as the manifold names 'state,' 'influence,' 'efficiency,' 'force,' indicate — something which cannot
exist by itself, but only as the predicate of another
subject; then the ancient proposition is valid, —
'*Attributa non separantur a substantiis.*' In other
words : A 'state,' and the like, can never be set loose
from the 'Thing' a, in such manner as to exist, for
an instant between a and b as the same state, but as
state of no subject, state *by itself*, and then subsequently be attached to b.

But, in the second place : If this 'passing-over' of
something were to be made a comprehensible affair,
still the only result would be, that c would now be
in the neighborhood of b; and the real question —

Why is this fact of such importance for b that b must change on that account ? that is, precisely how can c produce an effect on b? — would remain as much unexplained as before.

In general : The 'passing-over' of any element whatever, called c, from a to b, can very frequently be observed to occur as a preliminary and, for some reason, indispensable condition, — a condition without which no effect would take place in b ; but this 'passing-over' does not explain the process of efficient causation. On the contrary, the efficient causation does not begin until this same 'passing-over' has already taken place.

§ 43. The doctrine of Occasionalism sought to escape from all the above-mentioned difficulties. Since it is impossible to think of any efficacy as passing over from one element to another, this conception ought to be wholly abandoned, and the course of the world considered as a succession of events, each of which is only the occasion or signal for the occurrence of some other, but none of which really effectuates any other.

It is easily obvious that, in particular sciences, Occasionalism has a meaning as the demand of methodology, not to direct useless efforts toward a domain beyond investigation. [Such sciences are

those in which the investigation of the general
method of procedure that one element follows in
producing an effect on some other, — for example,
the body on the soul, — has peculiar difficulties. In
these cases, the only real fruit which investigation
wins does not consist in the solution of such a general
inquiry, but in the solution of the special question :
With what states of the one element (for example,
the soul) are certain states of the other element (for
example, the body) united according to a general law.]
On the contrary, Occasionalism could become a *theory*, an explanation of this uninvestigated domain,
only if it should succeed in demonstrating precisely
by what means an event **a** can be or become an
'occasion' for another event **b**.

§ **44**. The demonstration just alluded to has always been attempted in such manner that God has
been considered as the 'Reason' (Grund) of this
reciprocally conditioned 'Being' of things and
events. From the isolated finite being **a**, it has
been held, there could never arise a conditioning
influence upon another being, **b**, different from it.
Only God, as the Reason of all, could supply this
deficient reciprocal relation.

Now, in the first place, it is possible to say, that
God in his omnipotence arbitrarily connects with **a**

the consequence α, and, for this very reason perhaps,
with a second similar a, another consequence β.
Such arbitrary and unregulated interposition in the
connecting together of events has found no philosophical defenders.

A second opinion makes the entire course of the
world, down to the infinity of time and down to every
trifling detail of its content, to be unchangeably predestined by God in the entire succession of its events
('Pre-established Harmony'). Now, without men-
tioning other objections, we must at this point raise
the question : If God withdraws himself again from
this world, after its beginning, and if, with the beginning, its entire progress in the germ, is created ;
then in what does the security consist that the course
of this world is actualizing the predetermined events,
in general and in particular, in the order of succession enjoined, and not in one utterly confused ? The
famous example (Geulincx, and, alas ! Leibnitz, too)
of two clocks that, because of their first contrivance,
always go exactly alike without having any effect on
each other, proves nothing at all. For each one of
these two clocks can go at all, and go uniformly, only
because its own parts constantly produce effects on
each other according to a fixed law.

Another form of the opinion teaches a universal
hypothetical predestination : God has not determined

in special everything that is to happen, but has only determined in general that *if* a certain x happens, then a definite ψ is obliged always to happen. This opinion also is compelled to assume the conception of efficient causation. For if a Thing **n** is to be subject to the state ψ as often as the state x is present in another Thing **m**, then **n** must take some notice of x's being present, in order to be able to distinguish it from the case of x's not being present; that is to say, either x or **m** must have some effect on **n**.

Finally, a last form of the opinion asserts a constant assistance of God (*assistentia* or *concursus Dei*) by means of which he at every moment brings it about in special that, on a's having just been present, the proper sequel β originate. This theory, too, does not eliminate the conception of efficient causation, but contains it twice over. For in order that God may attach to every a its β, and to every x its ψ, it is necessary, in the first place, that the presence of the a or of the x, at the moment when one of them is present, have some effect on God, and that the existence of a have a different effect from that of ; in the second place, it is necessary besides that God, in consequence of the consistency of his own being, react upon the things concerned; and of course in one way to produce β, and again in a different way to produce ψ.

It would render no further assistance for the explanation of efficient causation if we planned to investi-
gate the relation C, in which a and b are absolutely
obliged to stand in order to yield a definite effect.

Universally C is assumed to be changeable, and the
effect arising is assumed also to change with its
changing.   C is therefore, to speak precisely, one
part of the reason which determines the content of
the effect arising.   A universal reason, however, —
one by the agency of which everything in general
actually originates, — would only be discovered in
case all such existing relations C, C₁, C₂, . . . could be
compared, and the characteristic common to them
all determined.   Even if this were possible, however,
the common character Γ which such an effectuating
relation would then have, would only be made good
as a matter of fact ; that is, we should be able to say :
two elements a and b can never have any effect on
each other unless the relation C between them is one
species of the universal relation Γ.   But *how* this Γ
brings it to pass that something actual follows from
all of its own species, while nothing follows from
other relations, would remain as wholly unexplained
as before.

§ **46**. The result of the foregoing discussion is as
follows : The conception of efficient causation is inevi-

table for our apprehension of the World, and all attempts to deny the reality of efficient causation, and then still comprehend the course of the world, make shipwreck of themselves. But just as certain is it that the nature of efficient causation is inexplicable; that is to say, it can never be shown in what way causation in general is produced or comes to pass. On the contrary, all that can ever be shown is, what preparatory conditions, what relations between the real beings, must in every case be given, in order that this perpetually incomprehensible act of causation may take place.

That the inquiry into the 'bringing-to-pass' of efficient causation is necessarily unanswerable, and in its very nature senseless, is shown by the *circulus* into which it straightway leads. For, if we want to get an insight into the causative process of causation itself, we naturally take for granted, as something necessarily familiar, the causal efficiency of that very cause which is assumed to produce the causation to be explained; we are therefore explaining efficient causation by itself.

§ **47.** Although it is impossible to gain any positive information as to the event by means of which causation in general is brought to pass, we must, nevertheless, at least in thought, supplement our conception of causation with all those auxiliary thoughts through which its content becomes possible.

Now, in the first place, the following fact is obvious: If a is to exercise any effect which it did not previously exercise upon a b that is now present, but was not previously present, or that is now standing in a relation C to a, but did not previously stand in this relation, then it is not enough that b *is* now *present;* on the contrary, a must take some note of this new fact. Dropping the figure of speech, all this means : there must be present in a a certain state a that is dependent upon the presence of b, — a state which is wanting if b is wanting, and which forms for a the sufficient reason of its producing an effect after having previously produced no effect. That is to say, in brief, in order that a may have an effect upon b, it must be induced to exercise this effect by being itself subject to some effect from b. Exactly the same thing is true of the causal action of b on a. The carrying-out of this consideration teaches us that every two elements which are to produce an effect on each other must previously have had some effect produced upon themselves, and so on, *in infinitum.* It is therefore impossible, in general, to speak of the absolute beginning of a reciprocal causation between ' Things.' The rather, — a conclusion that easily follows, — must the reciprocal causation of all things be regarded as an eternal, uninterrupted matter of fact. In the World causal action does not alternate with non-action, but it is only the form of the individual effects, within the sphere of unceasing efficient causation, that is changed.

§ 48. We remark, however, in the second place, that the 'passing-over' of an influence from one being **a** to the other being **b** is still assumed even in the above-mentioned mode of conceiving of the matter; that is to say, what is or happens within the one being **a** is considered as the sufficient reason why somewhat is or happens also in the other being **b.**

Now as long as **a** and **b** have the value of beings independent of each other and self-subsisting, — no matter how similar, comparable, or related their natures may otherwise be, — so long is the above assumption without a reason for its possibility : the states of **a** have nothing to do with **b**, and conversely. All the pains-taking, however, to bring these 'Things,' which are of themselves quite isolated, into some relation in a supplementary way, by means of ideas of the 'passing-over' of some influence, have been shown to be perfectly fruitless.

If, therefore, causal action is to appear possible at all, this assumption of the independence of 'Things' toward one another must be denied absolutely. A

state a, which takes place in the element a, must, for
the very reason that it is in a, likewise *be* an 'affection'
in b; but it does not necessarily have to *become* such
an 'affection' of b by means of an influence issuing
from a.

The foregoing requirement can be met only by
the assumption that all individual things are substan-
tially One: that is to say, they do not merely become
combined subsequently by all manner of relations,
each individual having previously been present as an
independent existence; but from the very beginning
onward they are only different modifications of one
individual Being, which we propose to designate pro-
visionally by the title of the Infinite, of the Absolute
$= M$.

The formal consequence of this assumption is as
follows: The element a is only $= M_{(x)}$, the element
$b = M_{(y)}$, etc. Every state a which takes place in a
is therefore likewise a state of this M; and, by means
of this state, M is necessitated according to its own
nature to produce a succeeding state β, which makes
its appearance as a state of b, but which is in truth a
state of this M, by means of which its preceding modification $M_{(y)}$ is changed.

Efficient causation, therefore, actually takes place,
but it takes place only apparently between the two
finite beings as such. In truth, the Absolute pro-

duces the effect upon itself, since by virtue of the unity and consistency of its own Being it cannot be affected with the state with which it is affected as the being a, without likewise being affected with the succeeding state in the being b, — a state which appears to our observation as an effect of a on b.

It is true that the manner in which it comes to pass, that even within the one Infinite Being one state brings about another, remains still wholly unexplained ; and on this point we must not deceive ourselves.   How it is in general that 'causal action' is produced is as impossible to tell as how ' Being ' is made.   The only meaning of this last consideration was to remove the hindrance which, consisting in the self-subsistence of individual 'Things,' makes the occurrence of this inexplicable process always *contradictory* in whatever the process itself may be supposed to consist.

Finally, it is to be remarked that the conception of the Infinite, or of the One Real Being, which we have here made use of, merely designates a postulate in a provisional way.   But the inquiry how we are to conceive of this Infinite itself, and of those modifications of the same Infinite which we explain the individual things to be, is reserved for subsequent investigation.

SECOND PRINCIPAL DIVISION.

COSMOLOGY.

SECOND PRINCIPAL DIVISION.

————————

COSMOLOGY.

————————

PRELIMINARY REMARK.

§ **49.** The common apprehension of the World is the result of the following assumption: A multiplicity of self-subsisting Things produces the changeable course of the world by means of the fact that this multiplicity stands in reciprocal relations: these relations change; and with every such change there arises a change also in the peculiar states of the Things.

Now the assumption of a multiplicity of self-subsisting Things was shown to be impossible at the conclusion of the Ontology. But even the common opinion would not strictly carry out this assumption. For since it made the Things be related to one another, and made them all together form *one* world, it obviously pre-supposed the self-subsisting existence of some background, or some medium, which is, to be sure, not real itself, but in which the relations of one reality to another pursue their course.

Now the question arises : In what way can such a background, a non-real form, exist outside of what is real,—a form in which, by its arrangement, the 'Reality' presents to our view a coherent 'world-whole,' a Cosmos ?   It scarcely need be stated, that Space and Time (and Motion) are the most essential of those forms, the consideration of which is incumbent upon Cosmology.

CHAPTER I.

OF SPACE, TIME, AND MOTION.

§ **50.** Metaphysic does not raise the question, — at least not at first, — whence our ideas of space originate ; but only what significance they have after they are finished, and what application can be made of them to the sphere of reality in consequence of such significance.

In accordance with the logical form of its mental representation, space is distinguished as an 'intuition' from the conceptions which we otherwise form of objects.

Every *conception* comprehends a general rule for the combination of certain marks, and requires obedience to this rule of every exemplar that is to fall under it. Such conception, however, leaves it perfectly indefinite upon how many, and upon what kind of exemplars it is itself to be stamped ; nor does it establish between the particular exemplars the slightest reciprocal relation to be of necessity followed by them. For what is called the co-ordination of such species or exemplars within the sphere of their general notion, is merely significant of the community of their subordination under this general notion, but of absolutely no other definite relation on the part of one exemplar to another.

Everything spatial is also subjected to such a common rule of combination, and this rule may be expressed, for example, as follows : Between any two separate points one, and only one, straight line is possible. But this law does not merely hold good for every single case of application, separately ; for example, for every single pair of points in such man- ner as to leave it quite doubtful how this pair is related to another pair that follows the same law. On the contrary, it is just this law which likewise combines all cases of its application together in such a way that every pair of points stands in the same relation of law to every other pair, as do the points of every single pair.

Space appears to us, therefore, not as a Universal which occurs in a certain indefinite number of exam- ples that are in other respects without any cohe- rence ; but it appears as a Whole which combines, as its parts into a synchronous sum, all the particular cases of the application of the law that prevails in it, in accordance with this same law.

This is the reason why the name for space chosen by Kant, — viz., an *intuition*, — is to be preferred to that of conception : there is only *one* space, and this space is continuously extant; all particular spaces

are only parts of this Whole, and are likewise continuously present.

§ 51. The customary opinion, for just the reason
mentioned above, very easily apprehends space as a
ready-made, .empty, and yet self-subsisting 'form,'
which precedes and furnishes a place to whatever is
real.

The conception of such a form, however, is not a
general notion borrowed from examples elsewhere,
and justified by means of these examples ;—a conception which could be used for the explanation of
space, because space might be brought under it.
The conception originated rather from the analogy
of space-containing vessels, which can pass for
'empty forms' merely in a relative way; because
some other material can be put into the space
included by them. But the vessels themselves consist of some real material, and are therefore not
'empty forms' in the sense in which space might be
called so. That the conception of an empty form,
which is framed by nothing real, but precedes everything real, is in itself impossible, follows from the
consideration of this very example.

Those other expressions, which style space 'the
total of the relations of things,' or 'the arrangement
of things,' or 'the total of the proportions between

them,' are all erroneous in that they do not at all express what we actually mean by space. For, in fact, space is not at all a definite arrangement, or relation, or form of things ; but only the *possibility* of all this : it is the incomprehensible principle, — in itself wholly without form, arrangement, and relation, — which makes possible indefinitely many different 'forms,' 'arrangements,' or 'relations' of things.

§ **52.** If space were actually a cohering totality of relations *between* 'Things,' then, for that very reason, it could not possibly have any existence of its own, independent of things and comprising or preceding them.

It is true that we are accustomed to speak of relations as though they could actually exist *between* things in such a manner as to bind together two of them without being themselves in either one of the two. This manner of mental representation, however, is quite obviously a simple consequence of our intuition of space ; for, by means of this intuition, it is impossible to represent under the word 'between' any mere negation of reality (any mere not-being) ; but it is possible to represent only a positive, intuitive kind of that distinct or separate being which belongs to the elements of reality.

Space itself, therefore, cannot be proved to have

an independent existence by an appeal to relations
which are held to have existed *between* reality, and
yet to have been neither a mere nothing, nor such
reality itself.   The truth is rather that space furnishes
merely the inducement to correct this false idea of
the relations, and to become aware that, in fact,
nothing can be outside of 'the Existent'; and, therefore, that nothing '*is*' but the Existent and its interior states.

Accordingly, if relations of space cannot pass for
inner states of 'Things,' but are obliged and designed merely to pass for external relations between
them, then it follows that they can only exist as
inner states of the spirit which is percipient of the
things, — that is to say, as forms of our intuition;
but they have no such existence of themselves as to
make our intuition a mere means for perceiving
them.

Finally, if what is said above is true with reference to all the determinate relations in which things
appear actually to be standing at a determinate moment of time, and therefore of the space-picture that
the world preserves at the aforesaid moment of time,
then it is yet much more true of the universal idea
of infinite empty space, which as such is merely a
possibility of relations.   Much more is it true that
such space cannot exist except as a mental picture,

which originates only in and for our intuition, whenever this intuition is reminded of that — occurring
in all its individual space-intuitions — which is common to them all and conformable to law.

§ 53. The above proposition concerning the 'ideal
character of Space' is established by Kant on somewhat different grounds; and it was used by him and
his school chiefly in order to make conspicuous the
perfect incomparableness of the true nature of
Things to the apparent form which they assume in
our intuition.

But such expressions as the following — "Space
is a subjective form of intuition which we set over
against 'Things,' and into which things fall only as
seen from our point of view, although they are in
themselves quite incomparable to all that is spatial"
— are contradictory; because, of course, whatever
is assumed to be able even to 'fall into' any form or
other, must necessarily somehow or other be com-
mensurate with this form : it cannot, therefore, be
absolutely incomparable to it.

On the other hand, we do not have merely the
empty intuition of infinite space; but we perceive
in space different phenomena at places which we
cannot perceive in another order at our pleasure, but
must see as they are. There must, consequently, be

a reason in the things which assigns to them these determinate places. That is to say, even if Things are not themselves spatial, and even if no relations of space subsist between themselves, still there must be other non-spatial or intellectual relations, which can be portrayed in general by means of space-relations, and which in special furnish the reason why, whenever they are apprehended in space-form by any intuition, each thing must appear to be at a determinate point of space.

§ **54.** If inquiry is made, In what do the 'intellectual relations' of Things consist?—then it would not suffice to look for them merely in the likeness or similarity, and different degrees of relationship and opposition, which belong to their natures. For all this is unalterably fixed for every two things; the spatial arrangement of the world would, therefore, if it be dependent only thereon, always be the same. But since things change their place, the reason for their various places must lie in the reciprocal effects which they exercise upon each other in a changeable way.

With the above assumption the inaccuracy of the expression cited in the foregoing article is likewise rectified; namely, 'intellectual relations' can as little take place *between* things as can other relations.

There exist only the states with which each thing is
interiorly affected ; and this is certainly not, as the
ordinary opinion assumes, by virtue of a 'relation'
between two things antecedent to such reciprocal causation and furnishing its reason, but is without any
media whatever.   It is not until after the 'Things,'
because they are all together mere modifications of
one Absolute, have immediately and without any
intervening mechanism acted upon each other, that
they appear to our thinking (if it compares this case
of their causal action with that of their non-action)
to stand in a 'relation' which conditions the action ;
whilst, — precisely the reverse, — their causal action,
if it is to be thought of, merely compels our thinking to place the ideas of things in another relation
than if their non-action is to be thought of.

Finally, it is self-evident that the bare reciprocal
action of two things a and b is no reason at all, why
our soul (c) should have an intuition of a and b in
general ; and still less in any definite order.   On the
contrary, it is only because a and b, by virtue of
their nature and by virtue of the states with which
they are themselves affected by each other, act upon
c (our soul) and produce in it the impressions α and
β, that the soul can be necessitated to perceive a and
b in general, and indeed, on account of the definite
degree of relationship or opposition which takes

place between a and β, to have an intuition of them in a definite reciprocal position. Whilst, at another moment when, by virtue of an altered reciprocal action between a and b, a and β also pass over into the new values a' and β', the soul will have an intuition of both in a correspondingly different spatial order.

§ 55. According to the ordinary view, therefore, space *exists* and things exist *in it:* according to our view, only Things exist, and between them nothing exists, but space exists *in them.* That is to say, to the individual being the other beings with which it stands, either immediately or mediately, in reciprocal causation, appear arranged in one space according to the kind and magnitude of the effect exercised upon this being by them, — a space which is extended merely within the individual as its intuition, and in which it assigns to itself a definite place.

Kant had understood the 'ideal character of Space ' in such a way as to make space only a *human* form of intuition ; other and higher beings may not be restricted to it. The later systems endeavored, on the contrary, to abolish this anthropomorphic limitation. They either sought diligently for the proof that space is a necessary logical result of the development of that total Idea which strives after its manifestation everywhere in the world (like the idealistic systems of Schelling and Hegel) ; or else they imagined to show how the apprehension of space must inevitably arise in every being which forms ideas at all, and combines manifold ideas with each other (like the realistic systems of Herbart and others). Not one of such deductions escapes the blame of having, in some manner or other, secretly smuggled in under the abstract conceptions from which it was to be deduced, the specifically *spatial* element of space, — the very thing, therefore, which was to be deduced. A decisive sentence, accordingly, seems impossible. Although it is very improbable that the World should appear to other beings as non-spatial and yet intuitive in some other fashion, still the necessity of the intuition of space for every percipient being does not admit of demonstration.

§ 56. We certainly do not by any means possess an immediate intuition of infinite ' Time,' but merely one that is obtained by help of the intuition of space, and, at the same time, in opposition to it. That is to say: When we conceive of a line in space, the points of which all exist together in like fashion, we gain from it a complete intuitive picture applicable to the precisely opposite case of time, whose line consists of points, of which each one exists only when the other does not exist.

The above-mentioned fact is aptly enough designated by the customary definition: Space is the form of that which has juxtaposition; time, the form of that which has succession. This '*succession*,' however, consists in a one-sided dependence of any two states of an actual being, a_1 and a_2, in such manner that a_1 is the condition of the actuality of a_2, but not a_2 of the actuality of a_1. If we represent the individual cases conceivable of the occurrence of this dependence, as summarized in one (of course, infinite) whole, and if we represent them, indeed, as following the same law which holds good for every individual case; then there arises the intuition of infinite 'empty Time,' every moment of which, on one side, depends upon one of its neighbors, and, on the other side, furnishes the ground for another of its neighbors.

Considerations quite similar to those in the case of space teach us that no substantial existence, however constituted, can appertain to time also; but that it must exist only as an intuition in the representative act of the spirit. It is not necessary to examine in detail the contradictions in which the two attempts to conceive of objective time involve us, to wit:—

(1) Motionless empty time, *in* which events elapse, is, so far as it is motionless, not 'time,' but another back-ground, on which, in order to elapse, the events themselves are afresh in need of *time ;*

(2) Elapsing empty time, which takes the events along with itself, can, in fact, neither elapse, since no moment in it is different from another, nor take the events along, since no one of its moments has any more relation than another to any one definite event.

If we carry out the above consideration we are led to the following result : Empty time neither *is*, nor *elapses*, *between* events or *before* them ; but, if the living causal action of 'Things' upon each other as arranged in definite one-sided relations of dependence become the object of perception for a percipient being, then in each case that which conditions must *appear* to precede, that which is conditioned to follow, and the total occurrence to elapse within the course of an infinite time.

§ **57.** The mental representation of the above-mentioned 'ideal character of time' is much more difficult to apprehend than the analogous one of space, to wit : —

In order to have an intuition of the supersensible relations of the manifold in the form of space, the

soul itself is in no need of space; or, — the soul can
bring forth what is spatial, as the product of its own
act of intuition, without its productive procedure
itself requiring to be spatial. If, on the contrary,
we say, — Relations of a manifold, that really have
no time-form, appear in time-form, if they act upon
a percipient being, — then we presuppose either, at
the very least this causal action as an event elapsing
in time; or else, if we should intend to assume that
this action also is a timeless impression, it still
appears as though our mental act of representation
could not posit one part. of the aforesaid manifold
as previous, and the other as subsequent, without
accomplishing the very act of positing the first, previously, and the act of positing the second, subsequently. Even if, therefore, everything that has
time-form were eliminated from the entire objective
world, it still appears that the act of intuition itself
would require time for the procedure by means of
which it has the intuition of that which really has no
time-form, as though it were in time.

To the above objection we now reply, that — quite
the contrary — we should never have a mental representation of that which is 'successive,' if our act of
representation were itself successive. In such a
case, to be sure, we should represent **a** first, and **b**
afterward; but only by means of a third act of men-

tal representation, nevertheless, should we descry the fact that these two representations followed each other *in us;* and for this third act they do not follow each other, but are comprehended in one synchronous intuition, — although in such manner that, according to its nature, a is placed before b as its conditioning reason, that is to say, as previous to it.

However extraordinarily difficult it may be to alter the mental habit opposed to such a view, still we are compelled to consider in like manner even our whole life, and the succession of events allotted to us as it arises in our recollections. We are not indeed denying that the aforesaid one-sided dependence of its constituent parts, which we regard as succession in time because we are necessitated to apprehend it in one mental act under the form of time, really subsists within that timeless actuality of which alone our assertions were made. We are merely denying that an *empty* time, existing outside of events and outside of our act of representation, is required in order that the aforesaid one-sided dependence may take place, or appear to us, as sequence of time.

Even the whole of our life, therefore, is a whole so articulated that all the other parts seem to stand in definite intervals of nearer or more remote relation to that particular consciousness which is filled up with one part of the same whole; that is to say, the series of states which furnish the condition for this particular moment of time, must appear to the consciousness of the moment as a longer or briefer 'time-past.'

§ 58. Secondly, an objection to the ideal character of time, fundamentally the same as the foregoing, can be formulated as follows : A happening or an acting that has not time-form is in itself inconceivable, yet must be assumed if we would intend to maintain the *appearance* in time of that which is really without time-form.

Now it is correct, that we, because we are once for all bound to the form of time-intuition, do always apprehend happening and causal acting as in time, and that happening without time-form is a contradiction of the usages of speech. But, on the other hand, it will be seen that the essential thought which constitutes the conception of causal action, — namely, the thought of the efficient conditioning of one thing by means of another, — does not require 'time' to validate it. That is to say : The existence or the elapse of an 'empty time' can never make any more intelligible than it would be without this, precisely how an **a** sets about it in order to condition or produce a **b**. As soon as the complete reason for **b** lies within **a**, then *time* can have nothing

to do with making the existence of **b** more easy or
more difficult. If, in experience, an elapse of time
appears to us necessary in order that the cause **a**
may bring forth its effect **z**, nevertheless time does
not in such a case work favorably by means of its
empty extension between **a** and **z**; on the contrary,
it is only because **a** is not the immediate reason for
z, but simply the reason for **b**, **b** for **c**, **c** for **d**, . . ., **y**
for **z**, that **a** cannot pass over into **z** except by means
of a series of intermediate states which is represented to our intuition as the filling up of a definite
duration of time.

§ **59**. We cannot define 'Motion' in a primitive
way as the passing through of a certain space. This
could be said only in case space were somewhat
objective which could be passed through, or the
passing through of which required to be made good
as a kind of performance or work. But space is only
an intuition *for us ;* and even for us not *primo loco*
an intuition of an infinite magnitude of extension,
but — stated accurately — only the mental representation of that coherent system of places which appertain to the different real elements, by virtue of their
supersensible relations to one another in our intuition.

'Motion,' therefore, means for us primarily 'change

of place.' To wit: If those relations between
'Things' (real elements), for the sake of which the
latter must appear at determinate places, are
changed, then the things must appear at the new
places which the sum of their changed relations
prescribes to them.

§ 60. If we added nothing further to what has
already been said, then it would follow from our
definition, that a thing ceases to appear at its old
place a, and begins to appear at its new place ω,
without having appeared in all the points between
a and ω,—that is to say, without having passed
through the distance $a\omega$. But such an event happens
only in fairy tales; in the realm of actuality, a thing
changes its place merely in case it passes over from
the previous place a to the new one ω through all
the intermediate places.

Made attentive by experience in the foregoing
manner, we recognize the incompleteness of our
metaphysical conception of motion, and endeavor to
supplement it. For this purpose, however, it does
not suffice to appeal to 'a universal law of con-
tinuity,' according to which a transition can be
made from a magnitude of one value (a) to another
of the same kind (ω) only by passing through all the
intermediate values. For, in itself, this proposition

is only a law of our mathematical imagination, and affirms : If two fixed values, a and ω, are given, then the difference between them is not arbitrary but is also fixed ; and, in thought, the a cannot be made to increase to ω, without adding the total difference $\omega - a$; nor can this be, without previously thinking of every one of its parts as added to a. On the contrary, the question which interests us, — namely, whether 'Things in themselves' are bound by the same law which our mental representation follows, is by no means decided by this method.

We look for its decision in the following way : the place a of a being a is fixed by means of its relation to b, c, . . . z. The reason for a new place ω occurs whenever the relation which previously existed between c and d is changed. Just so the reason for another new place ω' of the same being, whenever the previous relation between f and g is changed. If now both the reasons, last alluded to, for the new place of the being were fixed only by their qualitative content, — that is to say, in this case, by the situation of the place which they require to have, — then there would exist no principle of decision, in accordance with which one of these reasons, if they operated simultaneously, must be preferred to, or made equal with, the other. We are therefore compelled to apprehend every relation which fixes one of these places, not merely as a fixing of *this* place in opposition to some other, but at the same time as a magnitude of the force with which the relation strives to fulfil the demand made on it.

Now the same thing holds good also of that relation which fixed the original place a of a thing; it, too, must be apprehended as a magnitude which withstands the reason for the new place ω, and does not simply disappear when the reason occurs at ω, but requires to be overcome by it. This takes place only by means of the magnitude a vanishing through all the intermediate values down to the zero-point; and by means of the reason for ω thus increasing correspondingly until it obtains the intensity which, possibly, remains with it after the removal of a, and which now fixes the new place ω.

Now if, as a universal rule, the totality of the relations of one 'Thing' to all the others is the reason for its appearance at a fixed place, then all the changed relations, which successively occur during the conflict of both the aforesaid reasons, must also manifest themselves in an unbroken sequence of the phenomena of the 'Thing' at intermediate places fixed by these reasons. That is to say: The element moved passes from its old place **a** to the new one **ω** only in case it appears in regular succession at all the points between **a** and **ω**; and therefore (in the simplest case) traverses in space the length of the straight line **aω**.

§ 61. If motion is change of place, it would further seem to follow that it must cease of itself after attaining the new place which is fixed by the changed relations. This contradicts the well-known principle of mechanics (that of the persistence of motion, or 'inertia'), according to which every motion once begun continues in a straight line and uniformly to infinity, if it is not hindered. Of the correctness of the above-mentioned law there is no doubt. A direct metaphysical deduction of it, however, is impossible; for all the more general points of view, to which it could be referred back, are unproductive. For example: The proposition that the conditioned effect must disappear with the cessation of the conditioning cause (a proposition which runs counter to the law) is obviously not universally correct; since there are numerous effects which require indeed a productive cause, but do not require for their continuation a maintaining cause. But the contradictory proposition, — Whatever once is or happens, that just *is* and *happens*, and can never of itself cease to be,

but must be done away with by means of somewhat that is and happens of a similar kind — may,
indeed, express the fact ; yet it is not so lucid as
to be esteemed a self-evident necessity of thought,
or strictly deducible from other propositions.

Nothing else seems to be left but the attempt
to demonstrate the law of the 'persistence of
motion' in apagogical fashion as a necessary postulate. We pass it over to the philosophy of nature
to show that no motion or 'Becoming' of any kind
whatever could actually take place, that the length
of no line of finite magnitude could be traversed,
unless the effect, which the cause productive of
the motion brings about in an element by means
of a momentary action, is regarded as a velocity, —
that is to say, as an effort to traverse a definite
space in every unit of time to all eternity.

CHAPTER II.

OF MATTER.

§ **62**. In experience we meet with various sensuous images which we call 'bodies,' and in them all, in spite of their variety, with certain common modes of behavior, such as extension and resistance to the diminution of the space occupied ('impenetrability'), etc. These modes of behavior, when taken altogether, we can designate as 'the attribute of materiality'; and every sensuous image that has this attribute is, on this account, called a material substance. It is the problem of *Metaphysic* to show, in what manner certain of themselves supersensible, unextended, real beings, can furnish us with those sensuous images called 'matter.'

If it is replied to the above question, that what is aforesaid takes place because one and the same matter is existent in all these bodies, but that it is once for all time made the peculiarity of this matter to be extended and to offer resistance; then manifestly, on the one hand, the materiality is not explained, and, on the other hand, a hypothesis is introduced which were admissible only on the supposition that it had special reasons from another quarter in its support. For otherwise it is just as conceivable that 'Materiality' depends upon a formal mode of the combination of real elements, without these elements requiring to be alike as respects their essence. If this latter assumption is still to be made, it must furnish express grounds from another quarter for such an identity of all reality.

Finally, it is obvious that 'one matter,' or 'universal matter,' can never be spoken of as though it were barely *matter* and nothing further. Since 'materiality' is, rather, simply a formal attribute that presupposes a subject conceivable of itself to which it appertains, this 'universal matter' also must be discriminated as a concretely determinate essence from other conceivable but not actual kinds of matter.

§ **63.** The attempts at an explanation of matter can proximately have two distinct designs :

The realistic systems which seek everywhere for the *causal connection* of actuality, and accordingly inquire under what conditions aught arises, endures, and perishes, in their explanations arrive at special 'constructions of matter,' — that is to say, at attempts at comprehending how materiality is constituted out of certain reciprocal effects or activities of elements that are in themselves non-material but real.

The idealistic systems, which set their heart only on the significance that the existence of every individual has for the complete expression of the one comprehensive World-Idea, arrive merely at 'deductions of matter';—that is to say, they show that the existence of matter is indispensable, if the aforesaid World-Idea is to attain complete expression: but they do not tell in what manner this postulate is actually fulfilled.

A great crowd of attempts, finally, have not made this distinction between the two designs at all clear to themselves, and vacillate confusedly between construction and deduction.

§ 64. Kant's theory of the 'Construction of matter' contains, —

(1) the correct thought that matter does not fill space with its bare existence; since, in itself considered, the co-existence of innumerable things at precisely the same spot involves no contradiction. Although one portion of matter resists the penetration of another, or even its own disruption, still it does this by means of the forces of attraction and repulsion which it exercises on other portions of matter, and, as well, within itself from part to part; and it is on this latter exercise of the forces that even its own extension depends. But

(2) fault is to be found with this construction of matter in that it is never made quite clear who the subjects are which exercise the aforesaid forces. If that which attracts or repels, is itself already extended body, then it is not '*matter*,' but only the subsequent behavior of ready-made material objects toward one another, which is constructed by it. If the aforesaid subjects are not matter, then they must be so-called ' Things-in-themselves.'   But since Kant did not permit any kind of positive assertions concerning such entities, they could not be made use of in this connection; and the deficiency in clearness still remains.   Later adherents of Kant, like Fries, simply confessed that the subject of those forces is already 'matter,' and that it is incomprehensible how this matter itself comes into being.

(3) Finally: Kant, from reasons not to be pursued in this connection, had a special interest in having continuous space filled up by matter also continuous; and, therefore, in having the various condensations and rarefactions of bodies explained, not by the diminution or—respectively—the augmentation of the empty spaces between their alleged atoms, but in such manner that the larger space should be just as completely filled up as the smaller by the self-expansive matter.   Such a thing

appeared possible to him by means of the assumption that the two forces of repulsion and attraction
could increase or diminish in various proportions;
and from this there results a continuous condensa-
tion and rarefaction. On the contrary, it must be
remembered that the assumption of two opposed
forces belonging to the same subject in relation to
the same object remains an insoluble contradiction;
and, as well, that no insight at all can be gained
into the question, by what means a change in the
strength of one or the other force should be brought
about.

§ 65. Herbart's 'Construction of matter' begins
(1) with an accurate specification of the subjects
concerning which he is to discourse. Real beings
of simple quality and devoid of all extension, they
have positions in space that are mere mathematical
points. So far as their nature is concerned, they
need have no relation to each other, and do not, in
themselves, act upon each other. Still they can
enter into a certain relation to one another, in
which the differences of their qualities become the
cause of their reciprocal action. This relation is
called the 'Propinquity' (das 'Zusammen') of the
real beings; in what it consists is not systematically
stated. But after

(2) this effectuating relation has once attained this spatial title of 'propinquity,' the actual spatial meaning of this word is by a subreption regarded as identical with abstract ontological 'propinquity,' and therefrom arises the following assumption: Real beings act on each other only when in spatial contact.   Hence it follows

(3) with reference to the construction of matter: Matter cannot consist of real beings separated by intervening spaces.   For since these beings could not in such a case act upon each other, they could not possibly have any cohesiveness whatever.   But real beings, since they are unextended, can have no contact with each other; they would, if they attempted it, all fall together in a single point, and the 'matter' obtain no extension.   On this account, finally, —

(4) the impossible demand is set up, that the unextended real beings must be partly within, and partly outside of each other, in order to give rise to both the cohesiveness and the extension of matter. No theory has ever been able to make it intelligible in what way such a thing as this is to be conceived of.

§ 66. The fault of this last theory of the construction of matter consists in space being regarded, though in a concealed fashion, as an actually existent yet unreal *medium*, which can accomplish some resistance to the reciprocal actions of things, in case they are remote from each other.

According to our view, however, the remoteness of two elements from each other is only the form in which we behold the magnitude and diversity of those reciprocal actions of Things, upon us and upon each other, that have already taken place; and such a phenomenon, therefore, can neither be regarded as a favoring or hindering condition for those reciprocal actions on which the phenomenon itself depends.   That is to say, — briefly expressed: All real elements can act immediately at and from any degree of remoteness; and it is just by means of these actions that they prescribe to one another the places in space at which they are to appear.

Matter consists, therefore, of a multiplicity of real beings, each of which is of a super-sensible nature and unextended, and all of which, by means of influence acting at a distance, prescribe to one another the reciprocal position that belongs to each as a spatial expression for all its intellectual relations to all the rest.

Matter does not, therefore, continuously fill a space; but it consists of discrete elements between which there exist intervals where nothing real is found. Still it would permit of easy demonstration that such a system of interacting particles distributed in space, on occasion of its reciprocal action with other systems similarly composed, or by means of its reactions on an external influence of any kind, would exhibit perfectly the same sensible properties which we customarily suppose should be ascribed only to a 'matter' that fills up its space without any break.

§ 67. Concerning the conception of 'Force,' of which use was made above in an accessory way, what follows holds good : If two elements a and b fall into a definite relation C, then for such a case there always prevails a universal law, according to which a certain consequence X must originate (it must in general consist of some alteration of a and b). Now because this law prevails universally, we are able to transpose this achievement of producing X from the future into the present, and ascribe the capacity for it to the elements a and b as a property constantly inhering in them, — that is to say, as a 'force.'

The above-mentioned expression is not accurate. For this capacity does not belong to the a absolutely, but only in case that it stand in some relation with b. This law is observed in physics by

never speaking — when wishing to be accurate —
of the force of a single element, but always of
the force which two elements exercise upon each
other; in this way the fact is recognized that
force is not, properly speaking, a constant attribute of the elements, but a capacity for an achievement that arises in them under certain conditions.
The same fact is expressed by modes of speech
that are in themselves devoid of significance : The
force is said to be existent in a, but *latent*, and to
be exerted only under determinate conditions (conditions under which, rather, it first originates).

Further, the effect which arises between a and
b is also dependent on the relation (C) between
them, and on its alterations. Speaking accurately,
this means that at each moment there originates
from the sum of all conditions a force valid for
this moment; and at the next moment a fresh
force from the altered conditions. If it is assumed,
however, that, so long as a and b remain the same,
the form of their reciprocal action (be it attraction
or repulsion) is not altered without the intermix-
ture of a third cause, and that, likewise, the alterations in the intensity of this action are proportional
to the alterations in the magnitudes of the relation C; then this assumption can be expressed,
for use, as follows: The element a constantly

possesses a force that is invariable so far as its *form* of action is concerned, — for example, attraction ; but its *exertion* depends on the alterations of a condition, C (for example, the distance between **a** and **b**) according to an assignable law.

Finally, nothing at all hinders **a** and **b** from exercising a quite different reciprocal action **y** under a quite different relation **Γ**; or hinders **a** from developing a quite different action **z** in relation to a second quite different element **c**. Following the above manner of representation, we can ascribe simultaneously to the same element **a** the many forces **x, y, z,** . . . that are partially opposed to one another. A contradiction were involved in this only in case these forces were regarded as properties of **a** with an actual constant existence ; the contradiction vanishes, because each of these forces belongs to **a** only under certain conditions, and, indeed, each force under different conditions from the others.

§ 68. It were a conceivable possibility that the unity of one real Being, — in virtue of its synchronous relations to several others that, in turn, are compelled by their relations to still other beings to be at different positions, — were necessitated to appear simultaneously at different points of space ; and our conviction with regard to space would readily permit of this as possible without annulling the inner unity of this Being with manifold phenomenal aspects.   Nevertheless, such a thing as this were conceivable only on the condition that none of these phenomena, too, should maintain an independent existence ; that is to say, every influence which touches one of them must *eo ipso* touch the whole real Being, and there must never be any process of mediation required in order to transmit the states suffered by one apparent part of this Being to another part. — Of this truth there are three applications :

(1) For example, all bits of gold in the world could be regarded as locally different phenomena of a single 'gold-substance.'   But the experience that what happens to one bit of gold is altogether a matter of indifference to another bit remote from the first, teaches us that no unity of substance belonging to all gold is assumable, in any serviceable meaning of the words ; the rather that the individual bits of gold are independent real substances.

(2) It could be assumed, as was previously found of use, that there are unextended, definitely shaped, indivisible 'atoms.' If such a statement is not merely to mean that, in the present course of nature, cer-

tain very minute particles undergo no alteration, because the requisite conditions for this alteration are not forthcoming ; but if it is to mean that every atom is, according to its very conception, a unity of being in itself real and indivisible, whose simultaneous appearance at all points of a limited volume is necessary for reasons alluded to above: then it would be apparent that this assumption of its real unity does away with the advantages which it was designed to get from its extension and form.   For it is wont to be assumed that these atoms have one or more axes, at the terminal points of which their action is different.   But this is incompatible with the unity of the reality throughout the entire volume, and is only compatible with the assumption of a multiplicity of active parts which are independent ; and it is by means of the relations in the positions of these parts that the different properties of the different points give conditions to the total form of the atom.

(3) The assumption that one matter fills a limited volume continuously, while being likewise divisible *ad infinitum,* and yet before division does not consist of parts, but is a real unity, is impossible for the same reasons.   Whatever permits of separation from a totality in such manner as to be, when separated, completely independent and able to exercise forces

that are qualitatively the same precisely as those
of the aforesaid totality, — only diminished in proportion to its magnitude, — *that* must already have
existed in the aforesaid totality itself as an independent element, or system of elements; and such
totality cannot have been an individual being, but
must have been simply the resultant of a composition of such independent elements.

After all has been said, we come back to the
view which is the one now taken for granted also in
physics, — namely,

Every volume filled up with matter consists of an
infinite number of real beings, which in themselves
have no extension, but which, by means of their
intellectual relations to one another, prescribe places
in space that are merely mathematical points; and
these, by means of the sum of all their reciprocal
actions, effectuate both extension in general, and
also the form, cohesion, and force of resistance that
belong to the extended whole.

CHAPTER III.

§ **69.** On considering the conception of causality, it was found that the various real beings which underlie the course of nature, when taken together, must be, either directly or indirectly, comparable; that none of them need be a *Unicum* whose nature were disparate from that of all the rest; but rather that all the contents which constitute the nature of 'Being' must form a coherent system in which each of them has its fixed place. It was further shown that all real beings ultimately can only be modifications of one single infinite Reality.

Both these propositions we are to apply to the inquiry whether there is in nature only one Matter, or matter diversified into species.

If the term 'one matter' is understood to mean that there is one actuality, from which the apparently different elements in the course of nature actually proceed, and to which they return, in such manner that this (one) 'matter' is the unvarying point of transition through which the creative force of the Infinite brings forth the particular elements in time; then the decision of the question belongs entirely to experience.   Experience, to be sure, has hitherto not demonstrated a transition of the chemical elements into one another, or their derivation from one universal original matter; but at least a considerable diminution of the number of elements is not improbable in its view.

If, on the contrary, we should consider the individual elements as modifications — constant and unalterable in the course of nature — of that 'one matter' which, in this case, would have no separate existence at all outside of these elements; then this thought has no speculative value.   For it would only combine — and that in inept fashion — the assertion of the existence of the aforesaid elements with the thought (correct enough in itself) that all these elements possess a series of common properties, on account of which the conception of 'materiality' belongs to them.   Now it follows from the first of the propositions alluded to above, that, if we conceive of the totality of these properties which are formative of 'materiality,' as constituting the essence of a 'Thing'; then the nature of each particular kind of matter must always admit of being expressed as a modification or function of this 'universal matter'; but without such 'universal matter,' on this account, underlying *realiter* the individual elements in the form of a 'stuff' modified by them.

As a consequence, therefore, from all that has previously been said, we derive the following proposition : The one infinite Reality is *without media* organized into a system of specifically diversified elements.   But since its diversity must always admit of comparability, the diversified elements are equivalent one with another (of course, according to a diversified measure), in relation to one and the same effect chosen for the purpose of comparison.   Because they are ultimately equivalent, they always admit of being apprehended as mere modifications or functions of one and the same fundamental Essence ; and this essence, called 'universal matter,' can therefore serve as a very useful formula for the calculation of events, without signifying any separate real actuality.

§ 70. The order of natural occurrences must be considered from two points of view : first, inquiry can be directed toward the Plan which rules in the combination of things and occurrences ; and, second, inquiry must be directed toward the general Laws of procedure according to which each step in the actualization of that plan is brought about.

The very separation of these two inquiries, however, forms the essential character of a *mechanical* view of nature, in the most general sense of this

word as opposed to many more restricted signi-
fications which it has acquired in the natural sciences.

The principle of such 'Mechanism' consists in
the following truth: Everything that happens in
nature depends upon real elements which, even if
they do not belong to one 'stuff,' nevertheless
admit of being regarded as modifications of a single
whole, — that is to say, as measures comparable
with each other. Whatever the inner states may
be into which these elements fall by means of their
action on one another, the kinetic energies in which
the same elements express themselves are always
comparable with one another; and their alterations
are connected with definite mathematical conditions
(position, distance, etc.).

At every moment, therefore, at which two beings,
a and b, occur in a certain combination C, this cir-
cumstance furnishes the sufficient reason for one,
and only one consequence X; and, throughout, if
either a or b or C, or all together, is altered, the
alteration of the consequence X into Ξ, which is
necessarily connected therewith, admits of being
calculated according to an invariable law. That is
to say, in other words: No momentary state of a
being, when in combination with a definite sum of
external circumstances, can ever produce more than

one definite effect; and, conversely, every effect
that arises is just what ensues from those given conditions with inflexible necessity.

§ 71. Now, within the limits of this mechanical
view, a definite plan for the coherency of events can
be considered as realizable only in case the content
of this plan (quite apart from all design that might
be striving to accomplish it) is besides the unavoidable result of a definite combination of given
circumstances.

The whole of the course of nature is, on the
mechanical view, to be traced back with inflexible
necessity to the supposition of an original position
and original motion of the elements,—a position
and a motion which are taken for granted as primitive and not to be deduced from anything further
back;—as well as to general laws, according to
which this particular result ensued from this particular beginning, while from another beginning a
quite different result would have ensued.

Every more circumscribed example of development according to a plan, this view regards as a
single case in which, out of the general course of
nature, and fully accounted for by it, single groups
of its elements are arranged into a totality whose
cohering unity consists only in the reciprocal actions
of the combined elements themselves.

In opposition to the above view another is advanced, which discovers not impossibility, to be sure, but absurdity, in the thorough-going maintenance of this mechanical doctrine. From reasons which we are to estimate later, the thought is held to be insupportable that not merely some casual structure, but even a phenomenon which, like organism, obviously expresses a most significant idea, is assumed not to develop from within itself, but to be merely the inevitable resultant of many conditions in themselves indifferent to one another, and only co-operating as a matter of fact.

For this reason it is denied that everything in nature is the necessary result of circumstances; and the conception of an organic or dynamic 'impulse' is opposed to that of a physical or mechanical 'force.'

'Force' is always — in the way previously shown — a constantly like capacity for an ever like achievement; only with respect to its intensity is it alterable under quite definite conditions. 'Impulse,' on the contrary, is a faculty for very manifold achievements; and which of these shall be exercised at each moment does not depend, at least absolutely, on conditioning circumstances that actually exist, but on regard for an end that does not yet exist, but is impending.

Concerning 'force' the further assertion was made, that it is *compelled* always to achieve whatever, under given conditions, it is *able* to achieve. Concerning 'impulse' the assertion is made, that it is able to keep back a part of its effect; in other cases to reinforce or somewhat alter its activity,— of course, with reference to the goal that is to be reached.

'Force' was never known to pass over from one form of causal action to another without a definite inducement: 'Impulse,' on the contrary, begins its effects, starting from a state of rest, by means that lie within itself.

Now it is through its own action that the living totality to which impulse appertains, is held to define for itself its own form and the connection of its development; but the external real elements it employs as means in its service.

§ 72. Let it now be supposed that such an impulse of development were considered as the attribute of a single real Being; and let it be left undecided how this impulse were in itself possible: still the other question remains, namely, Under what conditions can it accomplish that which is ascribed to it?

If now one Being is to accommodate itself to the

changeable circumstances with a changeable activity,
in such manner that the latter is at the same time
always adapted to a definite final purpose, then it is
necessary

(1) that the Being experience some influence in
general from the aforesaid circumstances, and, besides, that the influence be changeable and proportional to the variety of the circumstances;

(2) that this influence in the Being itself beget a
reaction which is adjusted not merely with reference
to it, but also with reference to its relation to the
final purpose.

The further question now arises, In what way the
final purpose — that is to say, a somewhat that is to
be, but as yet is not — can be represented in this
Being in such manner as to be able to exercise its
co-determining influence upon these reactions.

From our point of view such a thing ·is conceivable only in case the Being either has a consciousness of the final purpose, and, consequently, the
idea of the purpose as a living state of this Being
is the force which can give conditions to the other
states of the Being, and so to its own reactions,
too; or else in case the Being works unconsciously
indeed, but its unconscious nature is originally constructed therefor in such a manner that the various
impressions which various conditions bring to pass

in it, undesignedly and necessarily combine into the totality of the development required.

In the last case, this development is quite obviously a perfectly mechanical result; and is not at all distinguished from the rest of mechanism by means of any peculiar principle of action, but merely by means of a special nature belonging to the subject which is active, and yet conditioned by the circumstances in a purely mechanical way. In the first case, the same thing is true, only in a more concealed fashion. For the *idea* of the final purpose, too, cannot determine the method of its accomplishment which the moment requires, *in a manner devoid of all principle;* but what accords with the purpose is discovered by a comparison of the purpose with the circumstances of the instant. Such comparison does not allow, so far as its result is concerned, of any arbitrariness whatever; and for the very reason that it takes place through the instrumentality of thought, it is positively in no less degree than other events dependent on the subordination, under general laws, of the contents compared (viz., the final purpose and the form of the circumstances).

§ **73.** All that is above-mentioned, however, would simply comprehend how, within the Being itself, a

definite purpose-full impulse can be awakened ; but
not as yet how this impulse can actualize what it
intends.

If now the impulse were to be directed only to a
succession of inner states in the Being itself, then
it might appear possible that a definite amount of
force for the forming of other states of the same
Being were communicated to it, in so far as the
impulse itself is one state of this Being.

If, however, an effect from the impulse is to be
shown in the elaboration according to a plan of other
real elements that are originally foreign to the
subject of the impulse (and this is the case, for
example, in all organic architectonic impulses such
as assimilate foreign material) ; then it is obvious
that the intensity of the impulse within the one
Being leads to nothing unless it meet with a like
obedience to its commands in other beings. Now,
since these other beings by no means experience of
themselves the 'impulse' to actualize the final purpose of the aforesaid first Being ; and since, rather
every being would naturally have its own special
impulse : therefore, a Being A cannot make other
elements, b, c, d, of service to its special impulse,
except so far as it can bring some compulsion to
bear upon them ;—that is to say so far as A can
exert forces that can be exerted in a definite mea-

sure by and upon every other being as well, according to a law common to *all* the elements. For every element **b**, **c**, or **d**, wants to be under the necessity of performing one of its own actions in pursuance of the same right as that to which it is itself subjected ; and not in pursuance of the particular preference of some other element.

The end of the above consideration is this: The conception of an 'impulse' adjusting the elements in accordance with a plan is undoubtedly permissible ; but an impulse never effectuates anything unless that which it wants is, in itself, already the inevitably necessary result of the conditions present at the instant.

§ **74.** 'Impulse,' accordingly, is not usually ascribed to one simple element, but to a combined multiplicity of such elements. And, indeed, it is assumed to be attached to no single one of them except in a partial way, so that it were the collective sum of the partial impulses of these elements ; it rather appertains to the totality of such a system, —a totality which, in this case, is thought of as in opposition to all the parts of which it consists. According to Aristotle, the Whole is previous to the parts, and produces, — not, of course, the real substratum of which they consist, but that specific form in them by means of which they are parts of this whole. To express the same thing in more modern fashion; the Idea of the whole is previous to the reality in which it is actualized, and rules it in accordance with its own final purpose.

It is scarcely worth the trouble to repeat that these expressions designate an actual process, but do not explain it. Of course the whole, or the idea of the whole, can be distinguished *in thought* from its corporal actualization; but it must then also be demonstrated, how and where in 'Being' this abstraction of the whole can exist as an efficient power and can give conditions to reality.

Experience shows — what can be known *a priori* — that an organic whole is never actualized unless it exist in the shape of a smaller and already extant system of elements, from whose combination and reciprocal action with external nature the subsequent whole must proceed after the manner of a mechanism. In this way alone does the whole exist as *potentia;* — that is to say, in a case like this, not as *power*, but as bare 'possibility.'

Just so, we can gain no insight into the manner in which an 'Idea,' that is in all cases originally nothing but the thought of a thinker, can become 'in Being' an efficient power; unless it, too, be first realized as a system of relations and reciprocal actions between different elements. This realization must be of such a nature that the development which we deduce from the 'Idea,' is, in fact, in this case too, produced *a tergo* by causes acting according to law ; and the development coincides with the Idea, only because its demands were likewise predestined as inevitable consequences in that reciprocal position of the elements which was given from the first.

§ **75**. According to all above-said, our entire view of nature would issue in thorough-going Determinism : all that happens would be the inevitable and blindly necessitated result of all that has previously happened ; and the entire history of the world would be restricted to the successive unfolding of a series of states, all of which lay already contained in the primitive state of the world as a future made necessary thereby.

The bare consideration of nature and of its economic coherency would furnish absolutely no inducement to alter this view ; metaphysical cosmology, therefore, concludes with it just as properly as the view itself everywhere underlies natural science considered as barely setting forth the facts.

If, nevertheless, our entire spirit is not satisfied with this view, the cause of the repugnance lies in the fact that, although in itself possible and free from contradictions, the view still appears incredible and preposterous when estimated in accordance with its significance and its value. Our mind wants that not all in the world be 'mechanism,' but that some One be 'freedom' as well; that not all be shaped by external conditions, but that some One at least shape its own being and its own future for itself.

Even in these demands of the mind there can lie concealed a certain portion of an inborn truth. In how far this is the case, and in what manner legitimate inference from our previous views permits of satisfying these demands, is left over for the last Division of our work.

THIRD PRINCIPAL DIVISION.

PHENOMENOLOGY.

THIRD PRINCIPAL DIVISION.

——◆——

PHENOMENOLOGY.

——◆——

CHAPTER I.

OF THE SUBJECTIVITY OF COGNITION.

§ **76**. In the ontological discussion we have spoken of the 'Being and States of the Existent,' without ability to specify precisely in what both consist. In the cosmological, we have taken it for granted that the world of phenomena as it appears to our intuition proceeds from these unknown reciprocal actions of 'Things.' Finally, at the conclusion of the Cosmology, demands of the mind were stirred that are to be prospectively satisfied only by means of an insight into that actual nature of things which constitutes what corresponds to the formal conditions of Ontology and Cosmology.

Now all inner states of all other things are unattainable by us; of only our own souls, which we hold to be one of these real beings, have we an immediate experience. Hence there arises the hope of learning from this example just what positively constitutes, in other things as well, their essential 'Being.' On this account the last Division of the Metaphysic could perhaps be called —as of old — 'Psychology.' But in this connection the soul is of essential interest to us only so far as it is the subject of cognition.

We therefore at this point resume the inquiry previously announced; after we have developed those conceptions concerning the coherency of all Things which are necessary to our thinking, — How must we now think concerning the nature and meaning of our own cognition, in so far as it, too, is subject to *one* of those same conceptions, namely, to that of the reciprocal action of different elements (in this case, Subject and Object)? On this account, this conclusion of the matter may be called ' Phenomenology. '

§ 77. From all the foregoing with reference to our cognition it follows, that —

(1) We recognize by means of no sensible quality an objective attribute of 'Things'; no such quality can be a copy of the Things themselves, but each can simply be a result of their influence. This result, however, like every effect, does not depend in a one-sided way upon the nature of the being which exercises the influence, but just as much upon the

nature of the being which receives the influence. Every sensation — as for example, color — is therefore only the subjective form in which an excitation of our peculiar Being, sustained through the instrumentality of external influence, comes to consciousness in us.

(2) Although no single sensation is a copy of the reality, yet definite relations with one another of the single real 'Things' seem to come to our perception in the very forms of combination in which different sensations are brought to us in juxtaposition or succession; and this happens in such a way that, while we could not, of course, cognize the single things, yet we could cognize the changeable relations between them. But the Cosmology has shown that the universal forms of Space and Time, within whose confines all the aforesaid special forms assumed in combination by the manifold impressions become specifically marked off, are themselves likewise only forms of our intuition; and it is *only we* who perceive in these forms the graduated reciprocal conditions of Things that are not in themselves subjects of intuition, but are only apprehensible as abstract conceptions. The World of Space and Time is, therefore, 'phenomenon'; the 'real Being,' which answers to it and produces it within us, is dissimilar to it.

(3) There, consequently, remained nothing left
for us but to maintain that only a *formal* cognition
is possible of the 'Being' of those 'Things' which
we proceeded to assume; that is to say, we were
able to define those forms of our thoughts by means
of which we defined the modes of relation belonging
to the unknown Existent, in such a manner that our
ideas of it accorded both with the general logical
laws of our thinking, and also with those more significant suppositions which our reason makes concerning the same necessary coherency of things.

Now the aforesaid logical laws, as well as these
metaphysical suppositions of our reason, are nothing
further than definite species and forms of its activity, which is excited by the content of the ideas that
are present within us.   That is, to wit: If, in consciousness, different ideas, a, b, c, d, . . ., are given in
all manner of relations, x, y, z, . . ., to one another,
then the soul is so framed by nature that this very
fact of a multiplicity of ideas serves as a stimulus
for it to interpret an interior connection into these
ideas;—that is to say, to regard the content of one,
for example, as the 'cause' of the content of the
others.

From this peculiar nature of the soul, in order to
explain the throng of ideas that are present within
ourselves, there ensues — as would easily be found

from carrying out the above considerations — the entire habit of assuming an external World of 'Things': and it is from the influence of these 'Things' *upon* us, that the aforesaid ideas are held to originate *in* us; while from their interchangeable proportions originate the given reciprocal relations of the ideas.

That is to say: It becomes at this point a matter for inquiry, whether simply the aforesaid most abstract and fundamental conceptions which we frame of 'things' and 'events' contain any truth whatever; and whether they, too, are not merely subjective habits of our own activity, by means of which a non-existent external world is mirrored before us.

§ 78. The above considerations lead at once to the view of 'subjective Idealism'; — to the view, namely, that all which we call 'cognition' is only a play of our own activity. The perception of the world is then a product of our creative faculty of imagination; the elaboration of perception by means of theoretical conceptions, and its interpretation by reference to a Kingdom of 'Things,' only a further carrying out of this activity, which still further articulates its product after it has constructed it. The same view holds, on the contrary, that outside of the cognitive spirit this world of 'Things' has no existence ; and, finally, that, so long as cognition consists in an agreement of the idea with its object, we cannot speak of 'a truth of cognition' in any thing like the ordinary sense, or even of an 'act of cognition' in general (considered as somewhat accommodated to its external object), but only of an 'act of representation' which is productive of its own subject-object (Fichte).

§ **79**. In opposition to the above view the following remarks hold good :

(1) The demonstration of the 'thorough-going subjectivity of all the elements of our cognition,' — sensations, pure intuitions, and pure notions of the understanding, — is in no respect decisive against the assumption of the existence of 'a world of Things outside ourselves.' For it is clear that this 'subjectivity of cognition' must in any case be true, whether 'Things' do, or do not exist. For even if 'Things' exist, still our cognition of them cannot consist in their actually finding an entrance into us, but only in their exerting an action upon us. But the products of this action, as affections of our being, can receive their form from our nature alone. And, as it is easy to persuade ourselves, even in case 'Things' *do* actually exist, all parts of our cognition will have the

very same 'subjectivity' as that from which it might be hastily concluded that 'Things' do *not* exist.

§ **80**. (2) The assertion that the World is the creation of his own faculty of imagination could not possibly be accomplished with complete freedom from obscurity by anyone except some lone individual indulging in philosophic speculation. Since it is quite too absurd that this one person deem the remaining spirits, too, in whose society he is conscious of living, as merely products of his own fantasy; and since rather the same kind of reality for all *spirits*, at least, must be credited; therefore the question arises: How do these individual spirits **A, B, C, D,** . . ., come to produce, by means of their faculties of imagination, four (or, if the case requires, **n**) pictures of the world, which have as a whole the same content, but which so vary in their particular features that the other spirits, **B, C, D,** . . ., appear to **A** at definite places, and they, in turn, to **A** at another place; — in brief, that all appear to each other in such manner as to make it possible for one to seek for and to meet with the other, for the sake of a mutual action in this non-existent phantom-world?

Obviously, the reason for such a noteworthy correspondence between the imaginations of the individual beings cannot lie in them as individuals, but must lie in some one individual and yet universal Power which is equally effective in all the individuals; and this Power — instead of first creating actual 'Things' outside these beings, in order afterward to produce in them the 'appearance of Things' by the circuitous way of an influence from these 'Things' upon the aforesaid beings — directly causes this same 'appearance' to arise in every one of them.

Idealism, therefore, would accord with the common view in this respect, that our perception of the World must have some reason outside ourselves; but not in this respect, that such reason must be sought in a multiplicity of 'Things' acting upon us.

§ **81.** With the modifications made above, subjective Idealism does, in fact, succeed in explaining the course of the world. Things would, of course, be no longer '*things*,' but only particular actions which the 'Absolute Being' exercises in all finite spirits in conformable fashion. But these 'particular actions,' k, l, m, n, . . ., since they are deeds of one and the same Being, would naturally so cohere, in accordance with the law governing them, that always, when k is exercised, the exercising of another act m also follows; and always, if the act k is altered to χ, then m also passes over into μ. That is to say, the entire coherency of natural phenomena according to law, for which we are wont to believe the existence of certain unalterable individual elements or atoms to be necessary as *subjects* of the events, is also possible, in case the 'actions of an individual Absolute,' constantly maintained or interchanged in accordance with fixed law, are regarded as substituted for such 'Things'; and as constituting a system of reasons — with manifold members and effective simply *in* us, but not extant *outside* us — that determine the content and vicissitudes of our perceptions.

§ 82. The above-mentioned Idealism, nevertheless, has failed to get rooted, not barely in the common mode of conception, — for which it is quite too much of a foreign growth, — but also in philosophy. It has been objected to it, that its so-called 'actions of the Absolute' could serve as a *substitute* for 'Things,' but still are not actual Things. That there must be *Things*, however, is firmly adhered to, from a motive very obscure and little analyzed. We want to possess in that Nature which we immediately perceive, something really self-existent and not barely a somewhat apparent to us.

If now the question is raised, precisely in what does that good consist which would be actualized by means of such a reality to 'Things,' and which the world would lack, in case only actions of the Absolute existed in its stead? — then it would easily be discovered that the bare objective existence, maintenance, and actual self-motion of 'Things,' and their actual but blind action on each other, would not have, of itself, in the least degree more value than the perfectly corresponding relations between the actions of the Absolute.

Precisely what we *want* is this, — that the 'Things' really enjoy these states of their own, and not merely be thought of by us as existing in them. That is to say, 'Reality' is '*Being for self*'; — an expression, by which we designate that most general characteristic of self-apprehension, which is common to all forms of *spiritual* life, to feeling, to representation, to effort, and to volition.

§ 83. Now if such is the exact motive for our ⸱⸱nce for the assumption of real Things, it ⸱⸱necessary merely to be persuaded that ⸱⸱o means be — as has thus far

been tacitly assumed — a certain species of existence called 'Reality,' which, wherever it is extant,
has there made possible the *'Being for self'* or
spiritual life of what is thus existent. Quite the
reverse, however, must we admit that to be spirit
is the only conceivable reality : that is to say, only
in the idea of spiritual life do we understand with
a perfect clearness what 'real Being' means ; and,
on the contrary, every as yet non-spiritual but
'Thing-like' reality is conceived of by us only
through the instrumentality of a collection of
abstract conceptions that make upon us the demand for somewhat more, of which we do not
know precisely in what way it is to be fulfilled.

For example : In the Metaphysic we have hitherto
considered 'Thing' as the 'subject of its own predicates,' or as the 'support of its own properties,' as
'substratum of its own states.' If now that one of
these expressions, which is perhaps the best, is analyzed, and the question is raised : In what precisely
does the relation, which the expression designs to
designate, consist ? — then it will be discovered that
only the Spirit or the Ego, which has learned in a
living experience to feel itself to be the independent
and sole personality in contrast with all its own particular excitations, has any knowledge of what it
means to be the *'subject* of states,' or to suffer and

to experience certain states.' In what way, on the contrary, a distinction of its own genuine being from its temporary states can be conceived of in a blind 'Thing' devoid of self-enjoyment, is quite impossible to see.

We have further required of every 'Thing,' — a requirement connected with the foregoing, — 'unity in the midst of change.' But how this requisition could be satisfied, and precisely where besides the series of its successive states this 'unity' might subsist, we do not know. It is the *spirit* that first solves this riddle by means of the miraculous phenomenon of Memory, which through a living coherence in one consciousness, of what is really successive, first reveals to us the only possible meaning for the aforesaid 'unity.'

We have, finally, spoken of the 'affection and action' of 'Things.' But these names, too, have a real significance only in case the 'affection' is actually suffered, — that is, consists in some feeling or other; and in case the 'action' is an effort or volition, and not a bare procedure of a result from a cause which thereat neither does nor suffers anything, or else is altered without any experience of it.

All endeavors are vain, on the one hand, to avoid assuming this character of spiritual life in Things, and yet, none the less, still try to say, precisely in what their 'Being,' their 'Unity,' their 'States,' in brief their whole 'Reality,' consists.   None of these words signify anything which, in its universality, were clear and comprehensible, and of which the spiritual life might form only a special example with other examples existing besides; but they are all abstractions which, from the spirit as their sole subject, abstract a formal mode of behavior that, in fact, is possible for its nature alone.   Thus they' induce in the unreflecting mind the semblance of an ability to signify something of themselves, and come to be assumed of all manner of subjects.

§ 84. The foregoing considerations lead to the opinion that there can be no 'Things' which are merely *things* in the ordinary sense of a non-self-existent, unconscious, blindly acting reality. Nothing but the following alternative remains : Either we ascribe to all 'Things,' as soon as they are assumed to 'be' *realiter* outside ourselves, the most common characteristic of spiritual life, — to wit, some form or other of 'Being for self'; or else, if we do not want to concede such an 'animating of all Things,' we must deny that they can be *realiter* outside ourselves.   For the conception of whatever has not Being for self does not admit of being distinguished in any tenable fashion from the

conception of a bare action, or a bare state of that
' Infinite Substance,' which we in the Ontology, and
in this connection afresh, have discovered to be the
foundation of all finite Being.

CHAPTER II.

§ **85.** After we have comprehended the unavoid-able and thorough-going subjectivity of our cogni-tion, and have conceded that we always see 'Things' . merely as they look when they come before our sight, and never as they look when nobody sees them ; and after we have finally reflected that this fact is no limitation whatever of our *human* cogni-tion, but must happen just the same in the case of every superior being, in so far as its cognition depends upon its reciprocal action with other beings, — then the inquiry arises : What kind of significance, ultimately, has such a cognition as this, which uni-formly misses of its object ?

We answer : The name 'Cognition' is the expres-sion of a prejudice, — to wit, the assumption that the course of mental representation which originates from external stimuli within the spirit has the prob-lem of reproducing in copy these 'stimuli' from which it springs.   In science our act of representation naturally serves, in every case, the purpose of ascer-taining a matter of fact ; but in the totality of the World it has another position.   It is a prejudice,

that the World exists, without the kingdom of spirits,
ready-made and completed in effective consistence of
its own ; and that the life of mental representation
which spirits lead is simply a kind of half-idle ap-
pendage, by means of which the content of the World
is not increased, but only its ready-made content
once more copied in miniature. The rather is the
fact, that a world of ideas is awakened within these
spirits by means of the influence of Things upon
them, in itself one of the most significant events in
the entire course of the world ; — an event, without
which the content of the world would not simply be
imperfect, but would straightway lack what is most
essential to its completion.

In brief : The mental representation of spiritual
beings is not designed to copy Things, which, because they have no such power of representation,
are inferior to spirit ; but 'Things' (so far as this
name has now any meaning left at all) exist *besides*,
in order to produce by·their influences that course
of mental representation belonging to the spiritual
beings, which, accordingly, has its value in itself
considered, and in its own peculiar content, and
not in its accord with an objective matter of fact.

§ 86. To give an example: We object to the faculty of sense that it shows us colors and tones which

exist nowhere outside ourselves, but are only affections of ourselves : it is therefore constantly deceiving us ; for the waves of light and sound which constitute what is truly *objective*, it does not permit us to see.

We answer : Such is undoubtedly the state of the case ; but color and sound are no worse, because they are simply *our* sensations. The rather do they constitute the precise purpose which external nature meant to reach with its waves of ether and of air. It could not accomplish this, however, of itself alone ; but for its fulfilment had rather an absolute need of spirit, in order that the latter might realize in its own state of sensation the beauty of shimmering light and ringing sound.

§ 87. 'The doctrine of the Identity of Thought and Being' (Schelling, Hegel) asserts, what is apparently the same as the foregoing view, and yet is really different from it, in more general form. The true Being of non-spiritual Actuality (the *modus existendi* of which is here left pretty obscure) consists simply in an 'Idea,' for the actualization of which it is intended. Only the thinking of spiritual beings, however, apprehends ideas as ideas. In thinking, accordingly, does that first become actualized which Things only in themselves — that is to say, in this

connection, Things according to their plan — really
are. It is not our cognition, therefore, that is unsuitable to reproduce the nature of Things; but
Things are unsuitable to produce their own nature,
that is to say, that for which they are intended. It
is thought which first makes them ready, as it were.

§ **88.** The above doctrine admits of a threefold
signification :

(1) If by the 'Being of Things' we designate
that by means of which the Thing is distinguished
from our idea of the thing, then it is quite certain
that this ' Being ' is not identical with being
thought. Or, conversely, thought is in no condition to comprehend precisely wherein the ' Being '
consists with whose manifold formal relations it
is itself employed.

(2) If again we use ' Being ' in the same sense,
and therefore as synonymous with ' being affected
and producing effects,' then the before-mentioned
proposition means as follows.: The thinking ' Being '
of Spirit is not one species of this Being, and the
blind ' Being ' of Things another species ; but the
latter, too, is a thought. That is to say: All that
we are wont to apprehend as the unconscious activity of Things, is only an unrecognized process
of thought within them.

(3) If we call that the 'true Being' of a Thing, by means of which it is distinguished from some other Thing, then this doctrine would assert that such *essentia* of Things does not consist in any Reality which is of quite foreign species and inaccessible to all the means belonging to the spirit; but it is rather perfectly exhaustible by means of our thoughts, or, at least, by means of thought in general.

§ 89. Herein lies the truth, that the essence and Being of Things cannot be opposed to the essence and Being of Spirit, as though the former were a second principal division of the world and a perfect stranger to the latter. So long, however, as the word 'thinking' retains the special meaning by which it distinguishes one definite mode of the spirit's activity from other modes, the Being and essence of things certainly is not identical with such 'thinking.'

In order to pass judgment on this matter one must reflect upon the exact share which *thinking* is wont to have even in the sum-total of what we really know. And on this point there is manifestly a very general illusion. To wit: as often as we in speech have designated anything with a *name*, the semblance of having constructed or pen-

ctrated the so-named content by means of an operation of 'thinking' arises in our minds, although
very often this 'thinking' makes a very small con-
tribution to what we mean by the name. — For
example :

(1) If we say, 'sweet,' 'blue,' 'warm,' then the
entire work performed by thinking consists in
designating by the adjective form of the name, as
though it were an independent property inhering
in another subject, a content which is wholly and
merely an experience in the form of immediate
sensation, but which can be neither produced nor
imparted by the medium of *thinking*. That is to
say : Thinking reflects upon the formal relation of
this content to others ; it does not exhaust the
content itself.

(2) Only by experience can 'weal' be distinguished from 'woe,' 'pleasure' from 'pain'; and
no operation of thinking makes it comprehensible
to a subject possessed of the greatest intelligence,
but of no feeling, what both names signify. They,
therefore, designate a content which is known only
if it is experienced.

(3) The same thing is true of our metaphysical
conceptions. What 'Being' signifies, no 'thinking'
makes obvious to one who does not from self-
feeling understand his own being. 'Action and

affection ' only that being comprehends who has in itself had experience of both. Even the abstract conception of conditionating were without significance for us, if we did not know from our own experience, from our own volition and effort, what it means for one element to have, or to have desired, a power over some other.

In pursuance of these examples we learn that all our 'thinking' by no means altogether comprehends, or in the least degree exhausts, what we could regard as the 'actual constitution' and 'inner Being' of Things ; and that it rather merely combines with one another in formal relations the ideas which designate the subject-matter of experience, whether in the form of sensation, of feeling, or otherwise.

§ 90. 'Being' could be posited as identical with such 'Thinking,' only in case the significance of the 'Existent' were so far degraded as to make the entire content of thought, which the actuality were called on to express, consist still in simply those formal relations of the manifold that logical thinking comprehends and judges of.

In fact, such is the meaning of Hegel, who not without significance calls that Logic which is elsewhere styled Metaphysic. If, therefore, things exist

and events happen simply in order that the formal
relations of Identity and Opposition, Unity and Multiplicity, Indifference and Polarity, of Universal,
Particular and Singular, etc., may be actualized in
the most manifold manner possible, and set forth in
Phenomenon ; — then, of course, the essence of
'Things' is so pitiful and insignificant that our
thinking succeeds perfectly well in adequately comprehending it.

§ 91. The teaching of Fichte had been different.
The problem of the spirit, he held, does not lie in
the cognition of a blind 'Being' (the conception
of which appeared to him as impossible as it appears to us), but in action. The aforesaid world
external *is* not, but *appears* to us in order to serve
as material of our duty, as inducement or object
of our action. Of course, the world cosmographi-
cally and historically determined, with which we
see ourselves surrounded, is not to be deduced for
human cognition as somewhat necessary to this
final purpose, but must be barely assumed as a
given matter of fact. Of those metaphysical principles, on the other hand, in accordance with which
we trace out an inner coherency within this phenomenal world, it can be shown that they are natural to our spirit on account of this, — and only

on account of this, — because the spirit is intended for *action*. For 'Things' considered as
fixed points in the course of phenomena, alteration of these things according to law, and reciprocal determinateness of them by causality, and so
forth, — all these are forms of the inner coherency
which a spirit, that wills to *act*, must inevitably
assume in that world on which its action is directed.

§ 92. The above-mentioned thought is not quite
satisfactory, because it makes all actuality exist
merely in the service of human action ; this action
itself however is only considered from its formal
side, as activity and self-determination, while that
content whose actualization were alone worth the
trouble of action is, on the contrary, neglected.

For the aforesaid 'action' of Fichte we substitute the morally Good, for which the action is simply the indispensable form of actualization ; we
besides conceive of the 'beautiful,' too, and the
'happy' or 'blessedness,' as united with this Good
into one complex of all that has *Value*. And now
we affirm : Genuine Reality in the world (to wit,
in the sense that all else is, in relation to It, subordinate, deduced, mere semblance or means to an
end) consists alone in this Highest-Good personal,

which is at the same time the highest-good Thing. But since all the *Value* of what is valuable has existence only in the spirit that enjoys it, therefore all apparent actuality is only a system of contrivances, by means of which this determinate world of phenomena, as well as these determinate metaphysical habitudes for considering the world of phenomena, are called forth, in order that the aforesaid Highest Good may become for the spirit an object of enjoyment in all the multiplicity of forms possible to it.

The .objectivity of our cognition consists, therefore, in this, that it is not a meaningless play of mere seeming; but it brings before us a World whose coherency is ordered in pursuance of the injunction of the Sole Reality in the world, — to wit, of the Good. Our cognition thus possesses more of truth than if it copied exactly a world of objects that has no *value* in itself. Although it does not comprehend in what manner all that is phenomenon is presented to its view, still it understands what is the *meaning* of it all; and is like to a spectator who comprehends the æsthetic significance of that which takes place on the stage of a theatre, and would gain nothing essential if he were to see besides the machinery by means of which the changes are effected on that stage.

CHAPTER III.

§ **93.** The view last approved — namely, that all metaphysical truth consists only in the forms which must be assumed by a world that depends upon the principle of the Good — can avail only as a consideration to fix the limits of Metaphysic, by whose instrumentality we assign to the totality of the principles treated of, their correct position in our total view of the world. But since those metaphysical suppositions, which we conceive of as dependent on the Good, are once for all the unavoidable habitudes of our spiritual organization, they are in themselves much more clear to our view, and certain, and, on account of their manifold application to the innumerable contents of experience, much more easy of accurate description, than is that 'Highest Good' which we conceive of as their source.

Therefore, although we apprehend the Highest Good as the one Real Principle on which the validity of the metaphysical axioms in the world depends, still we cannot regard it as a principle of cognition that can be profitably converted into a major premise from which to deduce the sum of metaphysical truth. Our presentation of the subject, accordingly, has no further problems to solve, which lie in this direction.

§ **94**. On the contrary, our further problems lie in the following direction : The very name, the 'Highest Good,' designates the content, the *essentia* of the highest principle, but not the form of existence which we must attribute ·to it in order to comprehend it as a conditioning cause of the world of phenomena.

In this respect three thoughts require to be united : —

(1) the thought of one Infinite Being to the necessary assumption of which Ontology led us ;

(2) the thought briefly developed, that no metaphysical reality can possibly exist except in the form of spirituality ;

(3) the thought just touched upon, and not further demonstrable as a matter of strict metaphysic, that the highest reason for the formation of the World, and of our metaphysical thoughts about it, is to be sought for solely in the Idea of the Highest Good, — Person and Thing.

The association of these three propositions yields the result, that the substantial 'Ground' of the world is a Spirit, whose essence our cognition were able to designate only as the living and existent Good. All that is finite is action of this Infinite. 'Real beings' are those of his actions which the Infinite permanently maintains as centres of out-and-in-going effects that are susceptible of acting and of being affected; and, indeed, their reality — that is, the relative independence which belongs to them — consists, not in a 'Being outside the Infinite' (for such a Being no definition could make clear), but only in this, that they as spiritual elements have *Being for self.* This 'Being for self' is the essential factor in that which we, in a formally unsatisfactory way, designate as 'Being outside the Infinite.' On the contrary, what we are accustomed to call 'Things' and 'events between things,' is the sum of those other actions which the highest Principle variously executes in all spirits so uniformly and in such coherency according to law, that to these spirits there must appear to be one world of substantial and efficient 'Things,' existing in space outside themselves. The meaning, however, of the general laws, according to which the Infinite Spirit proceeds in the creation, preservation, and government of the apparent world of Things, is to be found in their being consequences of that Idea of the Good, which is its own nature.

§ 95. In case we characterize — as was just done — an action of the Infinite as a 'consequence' of another nature, or of its own nature; and, in general, as often as we make that which is highest of all the object of investigation, there always arises the appearance of positing a 'kingdom of absolutely valid truth' previous even to the 'supreme Source of all actuality': in accordance with this truth would the decision be, what property b *must*, even in the Infinite, succeed the other property a.

The above thought has been expressly formulated as follows: A 'negative Absolute' — that is, an unconditioned truth (comprising the laws of Metaphysic and Mathematics) — does, in fact, precede all actuality, as a kind of immemorial necessity ('absolute Prius'); and it defines under what formal conditions, and in what modes, all must be, in case aught whatever is to be. Within these unyielding limits thus drawn, a 'positive Absolute' with freedom then creates an actuality which, accordingly, satisfies the formal conditions of the aforesaid 'negative Absolute' without originating from it so far as its material content is concerned (Herm. Weisse).

§ 96. Our previous reflections led to the opposite conclusion.

Over and over again were we made to see that no 'law' and no 'truth' can exist within the World, *before, outside, between* or *above* the 'Things,' concerning which it is assumed to hold good : law or truth is, and acts, only in so far as it is realized as a 'state' or 'activity' of, or within, the living Existent.

Still less, therefore, can a collection of laws already valid be thought of as existing in a perfectly void Nothing, before the World and God was, in accordance with which God directed himself in creating *this* world ; — and every other God would be compelled also to direct himself when creating another world !

Rather, the absolute living and creative Spirit alone *is ;* and He is the first principle of all in such manner that even the truth, according to which he seems to create, is only extant after his creative act.

That is to say : Since God unfolds the infinite activities, which become for Him and for finite spirits the object of knowledge, therefore, this knowledge can, on comparison of those manifold actions, comprehend the meaning common to them all in universal propositions. It is these propositions which, in the first place, because they hold good throughout the whole created world, admit of being considered with reference to every particular of the world, even when yet unobserved or still future, as rules by anticipation. And, on the same account, do they come to be considered by us, with an erroneous generalization, as a power controlling all the future and all actuality: just as though they were not merely the laws which, proceeding from the primal Existent One, hold good for the world that sprung from Him; but as though they preceded all actuality, and even that primal Reality from which they spring, like some inscrutable Fate.

§ 97. One must hold firmly to the above reflection, in order to avoid questions that are unanswerable; for example: How does the Supreme Being begin to sustain such relations to itself as to be a conscious Spirit? Precisely in what do those modifications of this Being consist which we assume to take place? How, further, does this Being begin to be at all, and impart to particular ones of his own actions that independence by means of which they become 'substances'?

At this point there is obviously a demand for explanations which depict these processes according to the analogy of those procedures by means of which one matter of fact follows from another

within the already created world. But every procedure or machinery of this kind is only conceivable in some such manner as combines into one
activity the already subsisting elements of an actuality already constituted in accordance with laws
that hold good in its case. Therefore, we cannot
be forever asking anew the question, By means of
what *machinery* or *procedure* does actuality in general, or its original matters of fact, come to be constituted?—for it is just from these matters of fact
that the whole possibility of reëstablishing any
machinery or procedure whatever is derived.

The supreme principles and the original forms
of their activity never admit of being 'explained,'
'constructed,' or 'deduced.' Our cognition, in
the most favorable case, masters only the interior
order of that manifold which depends upon these
principles. But how the principles themselves
have power to 'be' or to 'act,' is an unanswerable,
idle inquiry.

INDEX.

INDEX.

A.

Absolute, idea of, in Metaphysic, 7 f.; in Schelling, 8; in Hegel, 8, 20; the ground of Things, 72 f.; Things are modifications of, 86, 136 f.; negative, 156.

Actuality, belongs to cause, 60.

Aristotle, categories of, 3 f.; doctrine of whole and parts, 123.

Atoms, as elements of Things, 46 f.; 110 f.

B.

Becoming, conception of, 45 f.; absolute, 48 f.

Being, conception of, 15 ff., 18 ff., 27 f.; never mere position, 19 f.; never unrelated, 21 f., 23 f.; of Things, determinate, 26 f.; the Infinite, 73, 109 f., 154; unity of the one real, 109 f., 113, 119 f., 121 f.; *for Self,* the sole Reality, 139.

Body, conception of a material, 100 f.

C.

Categories, of Aristotle, 3 f.; of Kant, 3 f., 5; Fichte's deduction of, 6.

Cause, conception of, 57 f., 68; never single, 58; nor transient, 62 f., 64, 71; efficient, needed to explain the World, 68 f.; Thing as a, 70.

Change, conception of, 45 f., 50 f.; connected with state of Thing, 53 f.

Cognition, subjectivity of, 129 f., 133, 134 f.; objectivity of, 143.

Cosmology, conception of, 10, 77 f.

D.

Determinism, as a conclusion of cosmology, 125 f.

E.

Essence, of Things, 35, 38, 40 f., 45, 52, 114; as a law, 35, 37; applied to soul, 43 f.

F.

Fichte, deduction of the categories, 6; Idealism of, 7, 134, 150.
Final Purpose, in Mechanism, 121 f.
Force, cannot pass over, 62 f.; an attribute, 63; conception of, 107 f.; opposed to impulse, 118 f.
Fries, view of matter, 103.

G.

God, doctrine of Occasionalism concerning, 65 f., 67 f; the Highest Good 154; the Ground of all reality, 157 f.
Good, the highest reality, 151 f., 153, 154 f.

H.

Hegel, doctrine of the Absolute, 8; conception of Being, 20; deduction of space, 88; on identity of Thought and Being, 145, 149.
Herbart, conception of Metaphysic, 9 f.; doctrine of position, 22 f.; doctrine of quality, 28 f.; conception of change, 46; construction of matter, 104 f.

I.

Idea, as a real action, 42, 124 f.; as actuality, 145 f.
Idealism, of Fichte, 7, 134; its deductions of matter, 102; subjective, 133 f., 136 f.
Identity, of states of Things, 54.
Impulse, opposed to Force, 118; ascribed to many elements, 123 f.
Infinite, the ground of Things, 72 f., 113; provisional conception of, 73 f.

K.

Kant, categories of, 3 f., 5; doctrine of Things, 7; doctrine of space, 80, 84 f., 87; construction of matter, 102 f.; on Things in themselves, 103.

L.

Law, as essence of Thing, 35 f., 37; as necessary to Becoming, 49.
Leibnitz, Pre-established Harmony of, 66 f.

M.

Matter, conception of, 100 f., 105; deductions of, 102; elements of a correct view of, 102 f., 106 f., 112, 113; Kant's doctrine of, 102 f.; Herbart's construction of, 104 f.; unity of, 114.

Mechanism, principle of, 115, 116 f.; as related to plan, 117 f.

Metaphysic, definition of, 1 f., 11, 15; Absolute in, 7 f.; Hegel's conception of, 8, 10, 149; Herbart's conception of, 9 f.; divisions of, 10 f.; problems of, 79, 100.

Motion, conception of, 94 f., 96; change of, as defining Things, 96 f.; persistence of, 98 f.

O.

Occasionalism, doctrine of, 64 f.; cannot furnish a theory, 65; Leibnitz's view of, 66.

Ontology, conception of, 10, 15 f.

P.

Phenomenon, always of some Thing, 48 f.; the world considered as, 131 f.

Plan, as related to Mechanism, 117 f.

"Position," conception of, 15 f., 17, 30 f.; never without relation, 20 f., 23 f., enters into our conception of Thing, 31.

Propinquity, Herbart's doctrine of, 104 f.

Q.

Quality, of Things, 26, 28 f., 32 f., 34, 35, 37 f., 130; Herbart's view of, 28 f.; always adjective, 29; Simple cannot change their content, 32 f.; known only by experience, 148 f.

R.

Reality, conception of, 35 f.; as ideal content, 41 f., 42 (note); unity of, 48 f., 109 f., 113, 115; identity of, 53 f.; is self-being, 138 f., 154 f.; of Things, 139 f.

Relations, necessary to Being, 18 ff.; involved in Things, 25 f., 85; classes of, 31 f.; as explaining causation, 68; intellectual, of Things, 85; of time-form, 91.

S.

Schelling, doctrine of Absolute, 8; deduction of space, 88; on identity of Thought and Being, 145.

Soul, idea of the essence of, 43 f.

Space, 78 ff.; conception of, 79 ff.; an intuition, 79, 80; not self-subsisting form, 81, 105 f.; erroneous definitions of, 81 f.; not between Things, 82 f.; ideal character of, 84 f.; Kant's doctrine criticised, 84 f., 87; no deduction of, 87 f.; as filled by matter, 102 f., 106.

Spirit, as real Being, 145, 146 f.; the Highest Good, 151 f., 153, 158 f.

State, belonging to Thing, 45 f.; connected with change, 53 f.

"Stuff," conception of, 29 f., 38 f.; as related to essence, 39.

Substance, conception of, 30 f. (see "Stuff").

T.

Things, Kant's doctrine of, 7; ordinary view of, 16, 77; no unrelated Being in, 22 f.; true conception of, 25 f., 30 f.; properties of, 26 f., 28 f.; quality of, never simple, 28 f., 37, 130; essence of, 32 f., 36, 37 f., 42, 45, 52, 139 f.; unity of, 34, 71 f., 77, 140; reality of, 37, 130 f., 136 f., 140 f., 146 f.; law, as the essence of, 36 f.; an Idea, 42; states belong to, 54 f.; action of, 55 f., 58 f., 69, 70; never independent, 71 f.; no space *between*, 82; as modifications of one Absolute, 86, 114, 155; motion of, 94 f., 97; knowledge of, *in themselves*, 96 f., 103 f.

Thought, as related to reality, 42.

Time, conception of, 88 f., 90; no intuition of, as infinite, 89; relation to space, 89 f.; empty time impossible, 90, 92; ideal character of, 90 f., 93 f.; difficulties of, 90 f.

W.

Weisse, on the Absolute, 156.

World, in Space and Time, 131 f.; objectivity of, 134 f., 143 f.; and God, 157.

HEBREW LESSONS.

By H. G. MITCHELL, Ph.D., of Boston University.

It has long been the custom to introduce the beginner to some of the languages by simple, practical lessons. The acquisition of French and German, even Greek and Latin, has thus been rendered not only easy, but delightful. Instructors in the less familiar languages have, however, for some reason, been slow to adopt the reasonable method. It is not strange, therefore, that a text-book for elementary instruction in Hebrew, answering the wants of beginners, should still be considered a desideratum.

The author of the book here announced, after several years spent in instruction, has embodied the results of his experience in a series of lessons, by which, as has been abundantly proven, a learner can in a few weeks obtain a good foundation for the study of the Old Testament in the original. The possibility of this result will appear upon a glance at the plan of these lessons:

1. They are confined to the elements of the language.

2. They are arranged in logical order.

3. They are illustrated and enforced by abundant exercises from the Bible.

4. They require a vocabulary comprising almost all the most common words of the language.

5. They are supplemented by extended selections from historical books of the Bible, especially adapted to reading at sight, for which, however, the vocabulary suffices.

It is clear that by this plan the student is as quickly as possible made acquainted with the language, and placed in a position with comparative ease to become a Hebrew scholar.

Another point, hardly less important for beginners in Hebrew, is the typographical excellence of the work. It is printed with the utmost care for accuracy and distinctness, from very large, clear type, imported expressly for the purpose.

The book has been examined and cordially endorsed by many of the most competent judges, and is already in extensive use.

Retail and Mailing Price, $2.00.

GINN, HEATH, & CO., Publishers.

BOSTON.   NEW YORK.   CHICAGO.

PHILOSOPHY.

SEELYE'S - HICKOK'S EMPIRICAL PSYCHOLOGY; or, The Human Mind as Given in Consciousness. Mailing Price, $1.25.

SEELYE'S - HICKOK'S MORAL SCIENCE. Mailing Price, $1.25.

HICKOK'S RATIONAL PSYCHOLOGY; or, The Subjective Idea and Objective Law of all Intelligence. Mailing Price, $1.95.

HICKOK'S CREATOR AND CREATION; or, The Knowledge in the Reason of God and His Work. Mailing Price, $1.75.

HICKOK'S LOGIC OF REASON, UNIVERSAL AND ETERNAL. Mailing Price, $1.60.

HICKOK'S HUMANITY IMMORTAL; or, Man Tried, Fallen, and Redeemed. Mailing Price, $1.75.

THESE books discuss the most difficult and important problems of human thought. Though each is complete in itself, they pursue the following order:

The EMPIRICAL PSYCHOLOGY gives the basis of all physical and logical science.

The RATIONAL PSYCHOLOGY connects all science with philosophy.

The CREATOR AND CREATION gives the philosophy of all mechanical and vital forces.

The MORAL SCIENCE is already in the field of philosophy, and gives the basis of Æsthetics, Politics, Ethics, and Theology.

The LOGIC OF REASON frees empiricism from all scepticism in the attainment of a Being absolutely Universal and Eternal.

The HUMANITY IMMORTAL gives the Divine history of human experience from its origination to its consummation.

THE HARVARD EDITION

OF

SHAKESPEARE'S COMPLETE WORKS.

By HENRY N. HUDSON, LL.D.,

AUTHOR OF THE " LIFE, ART, AND CHARACTERS OF SHAKESPEARE,"
EDITOR OF "SCHOOL SHAKESPEARE," ETC.

---

*In Twenty Volumes, duodecimo, two plays in each volume; also in Ten
Volumes, of four plays each.*

RETAIL PRICES.

20-vol. edition	cloth . .	. $25.00		10-vol. edition	cloth . .	. $20.00
	half-calf	. 55.00			half-calf	. 40.00

HUDSON'S " LIFE, ART, AND CHARACTERS OF SHAKESPEARE " (*2 vols.*) *are
uniform in size and binding with the* THE HARVARD EDITION, *and are
included with it at the following retail prices: Cloth, $4.00 per set;
half-calf, $8.00 per set.*

THE HARVARD EDITION has been undertaken and the plan of it shaped
with a special view to making the Poet's pages pleasant and attractive to
general readers. Within the last thirty years great advances and additions
have been made in the way of preparation for such a work, and these
volumes bring the whole matter of Shakespeare up abreast with the latest
researches.

The first volume contains "the Burbage portrait," and a life of the Poet.
A history of each play is given in its appropriate volume. The plays are
arranged in three distinct series: Comedies, Histories, and Tragedies;
and the plays of each series presented, as nearly as may be, in the chrono-
logical order of the writing.

An obvious merit of this edition is, that each volume has two sets of
notes, — one mainly devoted to explaining the text, and placed at the foot
of the page; the other mostly occupied with matters of textual comment
and criticism, and printed at the end of each play. The edition is thus
admirably suited to the uses both of the general reader and of the special
student. The foot-notes supply such and so much of explanatory comment
as may be required by people who read Shakespeare, not to learn philology
or the technicalities of the scholiast, but to learn Shakespeare himself; to
take in his thought, to taste his wisdom, and to feel his beauty.

GINN, HEATH, & CO., Publishers.

BOSTON.   NEW YORK.   CHICAGO.

A STUDY OF THE DRINK QUESTION,

ENTITLED

"THE FOUNDATION OF DEATH."

By Axel Gustafson.   600 pp. 12mo.   Retail and Mailing Price, $2.00.

This book has already been accepted in England as the most complete work on the subject ever published, and one that will be "the Bible of temperance reformers for years to come." It is pronounced the fairest, most exhaustive, freshest, and most original of all the literature on the subject that has yet appeared. It is impartial and careful in its evidence, fair and fearless in its conclusions, and its accuracy is vouched for by the best physiologists and physicians.

In preparation for this work, the author has made exhaustive and impartial researches in the alcohol literature of nearly all countries, having examined, in the various languages, some three thousand works on alcohol and cognate subjects, from a large proportion of which carefully selected quotations are made.

The scope of the work, as to the variety of standpoints from which it is treated, is indicated in the following list of chapters: —

GINN, HEATH, & CO., Publishers.

www.ingramcontent.com/pod-product-compliance
Lightning Source LLC
Chambersburg PA
CBHW032010060726
47497CB00017B/2904